A Tradwife Tale

Also from EATMS Productions

Books on power, survival, women's autonomy, and the systems shaping modern America.

Nonfiction

Billionaires, Capitalism, and Power

Evil and the Mountain Ungreed
Self Help for American Billionaires
Selfish Steve and the Ivory Tower
Tariffs, Taxes, & Face-Eating Leopards
Ban Billionaires: Fascism Fix

Fascism, Religion, and Cultural Control

Self Help for the Manosphere
Fascism 2025
Fascism & the Perverts & the Greed Virus
Christian Fascism Marriage Book
Tyranny, Table Manners, & Tiramisu

Guides for Women's Autonomy and Protection

How to Survive in Post-America as a Woman
Project 2025 American Drag
4B – Burn, Ban, Boycott, Build
4B OG – So No Go GYN
I'm Glad He's Dead

Analysis of Authoritarian Project 2025

Project 2025: The Blueprint
Project 2025: The List
Project 2025, Christian Dumb Dumbs, & The Republican Agenda
Fascism, Project 2025, & The Pinkprint

Modern Rewrites for Women

Stoic Principles Reimagined
Siddhartha Reimagined
The Prince Reimagined for Women
The Art of War Reimagined for Women
The Jungle Reimagined
The Constitution Reimagined for Women

Machine Learning Series

AI, Bitcoin, Nostr for Women
AI, Safety, & Security for Women
AI, Anxiety, & Health for Women
AI, Kids, & Family Safety for Women
AI, Creativity, & Personal Expression for Women
AI, Independent Work, & Parallel Power for Women

Social Systems Series

Emotional Labor for Women
Household Power for Women
Workplace Power for Women
Medical Bias for Women
Aging Systems for Women
Recovery Systems for Women

Fiction

Dystopian Stories of Resistance and Collapse

Propaganda Paige & the Missing Prosperity
Propaganda Paige & the TIDE Manifesto
Propaganda Paige & the Shadow Cartographers
Propaganda Paige & the Prosperity Alliance
Propaganda Paige & the Shattered Truth
Propaganda Paige & the Rising TIDE
Propaganda Paige & the Last Bastion
Propaganda Paige & the Dawn of Prosperity
Project 2025: Dorian — The Last Men
Project 2025: Boy — A Last Men Novel

Christian Fascism Marriage Book: A Tradwife Tale

Apostates, Heretics, & Angels 1

by
Avisha Meḥomemet

EATMS
PRODUCTIONS

This title is part of an ongoing body of work. All EATMS Productions titles, across all series, authors, and formats, are components of a single connected project.

This book is a work of opinion and creative interpretation. While some names and events may be referenced or alluded to, any claims made are based on publicly available information and are intended as satire, parody, or commentary on societal and political issues. The content should not be interpreted as factual assertions about any individual or entity. The author does not intend to defraud, defame, or mislead, and encourages readers to form their own conclusions. Any resemblance to real persons, living or dead, is purely coincidental unless explicitly noted otherwise.

ISBN: 978-1-966014-21-8

Cover, interior design, interior prints by: Esme Mees

eatms@pm.me
www.eatms.me

Printed in the United States of America.

The woman who realizes that she is bound by a million Lilliputian threads in an attitude of impotence and hatred masquerading as tranquility and love has no option but to run away, if she is not to be corrupted and extinguished utterly.

— Germaine Greer

Table of Contents

Entry 1—
My Love Story Begins

I always dreamed of a husband who would cherish and lead me. From the time I was old enough to braid my dolls' hair, I understood that my purpose in life was to be a wife, to be a mother, to be a woman set apart for God's divine order. It was never a question, never a debate, never something I considered resisting. Why would I? My mother loved my father, and she loved God, and she showed her love through obedience, through quiet servitude, through the careful, unseen work of shaping a household into a place of peace and submission. This was the highest calling, she told me, the holiest work a woman could undertake.

The world outside of our home was filled with confusion, with discontented women who had been deceived into believing they were meant for more. I saw them, the women on television with their short hair and hard voices, arguing with men, demanding power, rejecting the natural beauty of surrender. They called themselves feminists, career women, independent thinkers, but none of them seemed happy. None of them glowed with the soft, serene beauty of a Proverbs 31 wife, the woman whose worth was far above rubies, who clothed her family in scarlet, who spoke with wisdom but never raised her voice, who worked but never led, who was strong but never dominant. That was the kind of woman I wanted to be, the kind of woman I was taught to be.

From the earliest years of my childhood, I was set apart. While other children were sent to public schools, exposed to evolution, feminism, secularism, I was homeschooled in the safety of our home, surrounded by God's truth. I learned math through the lens of scripture, writing through the works of Christian women who glorified their husbands with every word they penned. Science was simple: God created the heavens and the earth, and man was made in His image. There was no need for questioning, no need for doubt. To question was to invite rebellion, and rebellion was the first sin of Eve. It was her hunger for knowledge, her unwillingness to accept her place, that led to the fall of mankind. I would not make the same mistake.

My mother taught me how to be gentle, how to listen rather than speak, how to lower my gaze when a man was talking so as not to seem defiant or arrogant. She told me that a man's pride was fragile, that it was a woman's responsibility to preserve it. I learned that men were the head and women the body, that a body without a head was chaos, and a head without a body was lost. Together, in harmony, we created the perfect image of God's plan. This was what I was preparing for, what I was waiting for, the day when I would find my husband, the man God had chosen to lead me, to love me, to give me purpose.

The other girls in my community whispered about crushes, about boys they thought were handsome, but I knew better than to entertain such thoughts. A godly woman did not chase after love. She waited. She prayed. She trusted that God would bring the right man into her life in His perfect time. And so I guarded my heart. I dressed modestly, covering my body in loose, flowing fabrics that concealed rather than revealed. I spoke softly, practiced my cooking, learned the delicate balance of being both capable and dependent, strong enough to support a man but never so strong that I made him feel weak. This was my preparation for marriage, my training in godly womanhood.

I knew the verses by heart. Titus 2:5, calling women to be self-controlled, pure, working at home, submissive to their own husbands so that the word of God would not be reviled. Ephesians 5:22, commanding wives to submit to their husbands as to the Lord. 1 Peter 3:4, urging women to cultivate a gentle and quiet spirit, which was precious in God's sight. Every verse reinforced what I already knew deep in my soul, my purpose was not to lead but to follow, not to question but to trust, not to seek my own way but to yield to the path God had set before me.

And then he arrived.

I remember the first time I saw him, standing tall and confident in the church fellowship hall, his voice deep and sure as he spoke to the other men about theology, about the decline of Western civilization, about the need for strong, godly leadership in a world that had lost its way. He carried himself with the kind of certainty that made me feel small in the best possible way, a way that made me want to shrink into his shadow, to rest in the safety of his presence. He was not like the boys I had known, the boys who stumbled through awkward conversations, unsure of themselves. He was a man, a leader, a warrior for Christ. And when he looked at me, I felt something I had never felt before, a kind of deep, settled peace, as though everything I had been waiting for had finally arrived.

He was older, of course, as men should be. A man must have time to become wise, to establish himself as a protector and provider before he can take a wife. He had already built a life, already cultivated the kind of faith that could anchor a household. And when he spoke to me, it was not with flirtation or trivial charm but with purpose. He asked me about my walk with Christ, about my beliefs, about my readiness to be a helpmeet, a supporter, a wife. It was not a game to him. It was a calling.

My parents approved immediately. There was no dating, no wasted time on emotional entanglements that could lead to heartbreak and sin. This was courtship, a holy process designed to ensure that marriage was entered into with purity and reverence. We did not hold hands. We did not spend time alone together. We wrote letters, exchanged scripture, discussed theology under the watchful eyes of our families. Every step was intentional, guided by prayer, by the wisdom of those who had gone before us.

I remember the night he asked my father for permission to marry me. I was not in the room, I did not need to be. It was not my decision to make alone. A woman's heart can be deceived, led astray by emotions, by worldly desires. But my father knew my worth, knew what I needed. And when he came to me afterward, his eyes filled with love, and said, "He is a good man, and he will take care of you," I knew that God had spoken through him.

The proposal itself was not extravagant. There was no grand declaration, no public spectacle, no diamond ring that had to be measured against others. It was simple, reverent. He looked at me, and he said, "I believe God has chosen you to be my wife. Will you follow me as I follow Christ?" And I said yes, because there was never another answer I could have given.

From that moment on, my life was no longer my own. I was bound to him in purpose, in faith, in devotion. The world might say I was losing something, my independence, my identity, my freedom, but the world had always been wrong. I was not losing anything. I was gaining everything. A husband to lead me, a home to tend to, a life that would glorify God. This was my love story, and it was just beginning.

Entry 2—
The Proposal

I had rehearsed this moment in my mind for years, picturing the way it would unfold, the way it was meant to happen. No dating, no wandering through a minefield of heartbreak and sin like the secular girls did, no emotional entanglements that left a woman used up before she even reached the altar. That was the world's way, not God's. I had been set apart, trained, prepared for this. And now, here it was, right before me, the moment that would define the rest of my life.

He was charming, but not in the frivolous way of men who rely on meaningless flattery. He was authoritative, composed, carrying himself with the weight of a man who understood his duty, a man who did not second-guess his place in God's design. He knew who he was. He knew what he wanted. And what he wanted was a wife. Not just any wife, but a godly one. A woman who understood submission, who embraced her role as a helpmeet, who did not hunger for power but for service, for obedience, for the sacred responsibility of upholding the home.

We had spoken enough for him to know that I was that kind of woman. There had been no need for frivolous conversation or silly romance, none of the secular nonsense of finding "compatibility" or testing emotional waters. He had no interest in wasting time. From the first moment we were introduced, his eyes had assessed me, not with lust, but with purpose. His questions were direct. How often do you pray? What do you believe about the role of a wife? How do you plan to support your husband's mission? These were not the empty, shallow questions of modern courtship. These were the questions of a man who understood that marriage was a covenant, not a convenience.

I had answered well. I knew I had. I had been preparing my whole life for that kind of scrutiny, that kind of moment where my worth would be measured not by my ambitions, not by my education or my worldly achievements, but by my readiness to serve. I had spoken softly, lowered my gaze when necessary, smiled in the way my mother had taught me, warm but never forward, respectful but never disinterested. I had listened more than I had spoken, waiting for him to lead the conversation, to set the tone. And he had approved. I could feel it. The way his shoulders settled, the way his expression remained serious yet satisfied. He was evaluating, discerning, considering whether I was suitable to stand beside him, and I had passed the test.

There had been no prolonged waiting, no torturous uncertainty, none of the agonizing indecision that the world told women to endure while men toyed with their emotions. I had always found it ridiculous, the way secular women pined over whether a man would call them back, whether he "liked" them, whether he was "ready to commit." That was the problem with modern relationships, too much choice, too much confusion, too much emphasis on emotions and not enough on duty. A man of God did not hesitate. He sought out a wife with the same clarity that he sought out a mission.

So when my father called me into the room that evening and told me, in his steady, measured voice, that he had been approached, that my future husband had come to him first, as was proper, I felt the swell of pride deep in my chest. This was how it was supposed to be done. Not a negotiation between equals, but a passing of responsibility, the transfer of a daughter from one God-fearing man to another. My father was my first protector, my first leader, but that role would soon belong to someone else. And I was ready.

When I stepped outside to meet him, the cool air wrapped around me, and I felt the weight of the moment settle on my shoulders. He stood there, waiting, his expression as serious as ever, as if we were already bound in covenant. There was no nervousness, no doubt. He was not a boy awkwardly fumbling his way through a declaration of love. He was a man standing in the certainty of his calling. He looked at me the way a builder looks at the foundation of a house, the way a general surveys the land before battle. He was measuring not just my worth, but my willingness.

"I believe God has chosen you to be my wife," he said, his voice even, unshaken. There was no question in it, no hesitation. He had already decided. "Will you follow me as I follow Christ?"

There was no need for grand gestures, no need for flowery words or professions of love. Love, in the way the world understood it, was fleeting, weak, emotional. This was something more. This was commitment, devotion, a divine appointment. He did not need to tell me he loved me, and I did not need to hear it. Love was not the foundation of marriage. It was obedience, faith, and endurance.

I nodded, keeping my gaze lowered as I had been taught, though my heart pounded in my chest. "Yes."

He exhaled, a quiet satisfaction crossing his face. This was right. This was good. He extended his hand, and I placed mine in his, not as an act of romance, but of covenant. His grip was strong, steady, firm.

"You will be my wife," he said. A statement, not a question. And I nodded again, because what else was there to say?

I felt the weight of everything settle in that moment, the life I was leaving behind, the life I was stepping into. My childhood bedroom, the softness of being a daughter, the shelter of my father's protection, all of it would soon be behind me. My life would no longer be my own, my name no longer mine to claim. I would belong to him, and in belonging, I would find my purpose.

Later, as I sat at my desk, I wrote the words in the margins of my journal, feeling a deep, righteous satisfaction as I pressed the ink into the paper:

Women today are lost. They think they can be happy alone. Ha!

I thought of the girls I had grown up with who had strayed from the path, who had left the church, who had chosen careers and apartments and friendships over the security of a husband's leadership. I thought of the way they struggled, their desperate need to find meaning in things that would never satisfy them. Jobs that drained them. Relationships that failed them. A life with no foundation, no order, no holy purpose. I pitied them.

They did not know what it meant to be truly cherished. To be chosen, not as an equal, but as something set apart, something protected, something honored in the way God commanded. They did not understand that true fulfillment came not from chasing their own desires, but from yielding to something greater.

I knew.

I had been chosen. I had been set apart.

And soon, I would be a wife.

Entry 3—
Wedding Vows & The Death of My Name

Today, I became Mrs. Dirk Wilson. No longer me, but part of him. The name I had carried since birth, the one I had written in careful, curling script on the inside cover of every journal, the name my mother whispered when she prayed over me at night, it was gone now, surrendered, exchanged, buried in the sacred order of marriage. This was not loss, I reminded myself, but fulfillment. This was not erasure, but completion. A woman leaves her father's house and joins with her husband, her identity dissolving into his, her existence merging with the one she has been chosen to serve. That was the way of things, the way of God. I had always known this moment would come, but I had not expected the weight of it to settle so heavily in my chest as I stood before the altar, trembling beneath the veil, surrounded by the voices of men who would see me given, blessed, and bound.

The ceremony was held in our church, the sanctuary draped in white, the wooden cross above the pulpit casting a long, golden shadow over the congregation. There were no frivolous decorations, no extravagant flourishes to distract from the holiness of the occasion. The beauty was in the order, in the reverence, in the perfect structure of obedience that defined every moment. The men sat in the front rows, the elders with their Bibles open on their laps, nodding approvingly as the pastor spoke. The women sat behind them, silent, hands folded in their laps, watching as I stepped toward the altar where my future was waiting.

My father walked beside me, his grip firm around my arm, his presence a steadying force as we moved down the aisle. He did not ask if I was nervous, did not whisper words of reassurance or encouragement. There was no need. This was duty, not sentimentality. His role was to deliver me to the next man who would guide me, to complete the transfer of authority that had been ordained long before I was born. And so we walked, past the faces of those who had watched me grow, who had seen me blossom from a quiet girl into a woman prepared for her calling. I kept my eyes low, focused on the steps ahead, on the man waiting at the altar, on the moment that would change everything.

He stood tall, unwavering, his expression solemn and sure. He did not smile, did not fidget or glance nervously around the room like the grooms in secular weddings, those weak men who approached marriage with hesitation instead of certainty. He was confident, as he should be. He was not merely taking a wife, he was taking responsibility for a household, for a woman who would look to him for direction, for children who would one day follow in his steps. His duty was weighty, and he bore it with the strength of a man who understood what God required of him. I saw that strength in his eyes, in the way he stood, in the way he extended his hand to receive me. And in that moment, I wanted nothing more than to be worthy of it.

The pastor spoke, his voice deep and commanding, filling the sanctuary with words that had been spoken over countless brides before me. Marriage was a covenant, he said, not a contract, not a partnership built on fleeting emotions or earthly desires. It was a reflection of God's divine order, a mirror of Christ's relationship with His church. A man rules with love, and a woman serves with joy. This was the foundation of our union, the cornerstone upon which our future would be built. I nodded as he spoke, absorbing each word, letting them settle into my bones.

He turned to my husband first, instructing him in the duties he must now undertake. To lead with wisdom, to correct with gentleness, to love with the firm, unwavering hand of authority. A wife is a garden, the pastor said, a reflection of the care given to her by her husband. A good man cultivates his wife, prunes away her weaknesses, shapes her into a woman who glorifies God through her obedience. My husband listened intently, his jaw set, his hands clasped before him, absorbing each instruction as if they were law, because in many ways, they were.

Then the pastor turned to me, his gaze sharp, assessing, as if to confirm that I was prepared for the charge I was about to accept. A wife is not her own, he said. She is given, she is received, she is covered. The world would tell women that marriage is a balance of power, that they must protect their independence, their autonomy, their ambitions. But the world is wrong. A woman's highest calling is not in leadership, not in personal achievement, not in the pursuit of her own desires. It is in surrender. It is in trust. It is in the quiet, steady work of submission.

I swallowed hard, pressing my hands together, nodding in agreement as he continued.

The vows were not like the ones I had heard in movies, not the shallow, emotional promises of worldly unions. There was no talk of equal partnership, of personal happiness, of whimsical love. Love was not an emotion here, not something that could fade or change with time. It was a duty. A choice. A commandment.

He spoke first, his voice steady, his words strong.

"I take you as my wife, my helpmeet, my partner in obedience to God. I will lead you, correct you, provide for you, and protect you. I will love you as Christ loves the church, with firm authority and unwavering commitment. Your burdens are mine, your life is mine. You will submit to me as I submit to Christ, and together we will build a household that glorifies God."

The words settled into my chest, anchoring me. There was no question of his role. No doubt. No hesitation. He was to lead, and I was to follow. He was to shape, and I was to be molded. And I was ready.

When it was my turn, I lifted my eyes to meet his, my voice soft but sure.

"I take you as my husband, my head, my covering. I will follow where you lead, submit where you command, and trust in your wisdom as you trust in God. I will serve you, honor you, obey you, and build a home that reflects the beauty of biblical womanhood. My life is yours, my heart is yours, my obedience is yours. Where you go, I will go, and where you stay, I will stay."

There was silence after I spoke, the weight of my words settling over the congregation. The pastor nodded approvingly, and my husband gave the smallest incline of his head, a flicker of satisfaction in his otherwise serious expression. The words had been spoken, the vows sealed.

A wife is not her own. She is given, she is received, she is covered.

I closed my eyes as the final prayer was spoken over us, as the pastor's hands rested on our heads, as the voices of the men in the room rose in agreement, blessing our union, sealing our covenant.

When I opened them again, I was no longer who I had been. I was not my father's daughter.

I was not the girl I had once been.
I was Mrs. Dirk Wilson.

And I belonged to him.

When the ceremony ended, the pastor announced our union with the solemnity of a decree, his voice carrying the weight of finality. There was no applause, no sentimental weeping, no triumphant outburst of joy. That was not the way of things. Marriage was not a performance, not a spectacle meant to elicit gasps and tears from an audience. It was a covenant, a binding, a shift in identity as significant as birth or death. And now, I was no longer who I had been before stepping into that church. I was his, sealed with vows that were not meant to be broken, with a name that was no longer my own.

As we stepped away from the altar, I did not walk beside him as an equal but followed half a step behind, mirroring the image of the church trailing after Christ. My hands trembled at my sides, though whether from excitement or something else, I could not be sure. My veil still hung over me like a sheer partition, blurring my vision, obscuring the faces of the women in the congregation as they watched with quiet reverence. There was no rowdy celebration, no jubilant tossing of flowers, no giddy laughter. The atmosphere was heavy with expectation, with a collective understanding that I was now stepping into the next, most important phase of my life. I was no longer a daughter, no longer a girl, no longer my own.

The reception was held in the church hall, a modest gathering without music, without alcohol, without excess. There were no clinking glasses urging us to kiss, no playful toasts about how we met, no wild dancing beneath strings of twinkling lights. Marriage was not about indulgence or extravagance, and there was no place for the frivolities of the world in a union meant to honor God. Instead, the men gathered in their own circle, talking of theology, of discipline, of leadership, while the women surrounded me, their voices hushed but insistent, their words heavy with approval and warning alike.

"You have done well," an older woman said, placing a firm hand on my arm, her fingers pressing deep into my skin. Her face was lined with the quiet endurance of a life lived in obedience, her hair pinned neatly beneath a lace covering. "You have chosen the path of righteousness, and God will bless you for it."

Another woman nodded. "A man like him requires a wife who is steadfast, who does not falter. You must be strong in your submission, unwavering in your service. If you honor him, he will provide, and your household will be blessed."

Their eyes gleamed with a mixture of approval and expectation, as though I had passed the first test but still had a lifetime of examinations ahead. I nodded, absorbing their words, letting them settle into me like stones sinking to the bottom of a deep well. I had always known this was what I was meant for, but now that I stood among them, a married woman, a wife, I felt a strange sensation creeping into my chest, a flutter of something that did not yet have a name. Not fear. Not regret. Just a sudden, sharp awareness that everything was different now, that there was no undoing what had been done.

I glanced at my husband across the room, watching the way he spoke, the way the other men listened when he did. His voice was calm, measured, the voice of a man who would not be questioned, who would not be challenged. I belonged to him now. Every part of me, my time, my thoughts, my body, my name, was no longer my own but his to mold, to shape, to lead. It was right. It was biblical. It was what I had always wanted.

But as I stood there, the weight of my new name pressing down on me like the veil still draped over my hair, I could not ignore the quiet truth threading itself through my thoughts.

I did not yet know who I was without the name I had given up.

The evening passed in a haze of quiet conversation, of knowing glances from the older wives, of men clapping my husband on the back with murmured assurances that he had chosen well. And then, finally, it was time to leave. There were no long goodbyes, no lingering embraces with my parents, no sentimental parting words. That was not the way of things. A woman left her father's house and became one with her husband. There was no room for divided loyalties, for looking back. My mother squeezed my hands once before stepping aside, my father nodding his approval without a word. They had done their part. Now it was my turn.

The car ride home was quiet, the air between us thick with expectation. My hands rested in my lap, my fingers curled tightly around the fabric of my dress, my mind racing with everything I had been taught, with everything that was to come. I knew my role. I knew what was expected. A wife does not deny her husband. A wife does not hesitate. A wife does not belong to herself.

As we pulled up to the house that was now my home, I took a deep breath, steadying myself. This was what I had been waiting for, what I had been preparing for. And yet, for the first time in my life, a whisper of uncertainty coiled itself around my thoughts.

I had been given away.

I had been received.

I had been covered.

And now, I was his. Completely, irrevocably, forever.

Entry 4—
My New Home

The house stood at the end of a long, winding road, set apart from the world as if it had been deliberately placed beyond the reach of anything that might corrupt it. It wasn't large or ostentatious, not one of those gleaming suburban homes with wide-open windows and neatly trimmed hedges where neighbors could wave and call out friendly greetings. No, this house was different. It was practical, sturdy, built for function, not comfort. The windows were shuttered most of the time, the curtains drawn, the rooms dim even in the middle of the day. It was a home that held itself inward, as if guarding against unseen threats, as if the outside world had nothing to offer but danger. It was, as my husband had said with quiet pride, a place where God's order reigned.

I had expected this, of course. He had spoken about it often in the months leading up to our marriage, about how a man must be the gatekeeper of his home, how the world was filled with wickedness and distractions that led women astray, that pulled children into rebellion, that weakened men into passivity. A Christian home had to be a fortress, not merely a dwelling. It had to be a place where God's law ruled, where secular influences could not seep through the cracks. The world outside was fallen, depraved, obsessed with pleasure and sin. He had made it clear that it was not just his right but his duty to ensure that none of it entered our house.

And so there was no television. That had been one of the first things I noticed, though I hadn't expected there to be one. Television was a tool of deception, a machine built to erode faith, to fill minds with godless ideas disguised as entertainment. It wasn't just about avoiding the obvious things, violence, sex, blasphemy, it was about something deeper. Television, he had said, made people lazy. It encouraged passivity, weakened the mind, allowed dangerous ideologies to take root. Even Christian programming could not be trusted. So there was no need for it, no place for it in our home.

Books were another matter. I had always loved reading, had spent much of my girlhood with my nose buried in pages, losing myself in stories of faraway places, of women who lived lives so unlike my own. But the bookshelves in our home held only what was necessary. Bibles, commentaries, devotionals. Books on theology, on biblical womanhood, on discipline and order. There were no novels, no works of fiction, nothing that might stir imagination in the wrong direction. "Fiction is a distraction," my husband told me when I asked about it. "It leads the mind into vanity, into unrealistic expectations. A woman does not need stories. She needs truth."

The shelves reflected that conviction. There were books on submission, on modesty, on how to be a godly wife and mother. Volumes about the roles of men and women, carefully outlining the divine hierarchy that governed all things. No secular authors, no voices outside of our faith, nothing that might introduce questions where there should only be certainty. The walls of the home were lined with scripture, verses framed and displayed in elegant calligraphy, each one a reminder of my place, my duty.

There was no internet, no social media, no easy way to reach beyond the borders of our life. "What could you possibly need from out there?" he asked when I timidly inquired about it. I had been accustomed to emailing my family, to reading articles, to browsing through homemaking websites for recipes or advice, and for a moment, I had foolishly believed that those small habits might continue after marriage. But he had only shaken his head. "That world is not our world, and you have no need to bring its noise into our home."

I had nodded, accepting the decision as right, as necessary. If I was honest with myself, I had already known what his answer would be. I had already understood that my life had narrowed, that the wide horizon I had once been able to glimpse, however briefly, had now been pulled away like a curtain snapping shut. It should have comforted me, this retreat from the chaos of modern life, from the corruption of the secular world. And in some ways, it did. There was peace in silence, in the absence of voices vying for attention, in the purity of a life without distractions.

But there was also a quiet unease, one I could not yet name.

I had spent my whole life preparing for this, for the moment when I would take my place beneath my husband's authority, when I would embrace the role I had been created for. I had known that marriage would require me to submit, to surrender my own thoughts and desires in favor of something greater. And I had believed that when the moment came, when I stepped into this life, I would feel complete. Whole. That submission would feel like a warm embrace rather than a door quietly locking behind me.

The rules of the house were simple, clear, unwavering. My husband had made them known on our first night together, not as demands but as truths, as principles that would guide our home in righteousness. "God's order is not a burden," he told me, sitting across from me at our modest kitchen table, his hands folded together in quiet authority. "It is a gift. It is the structure that keeps us safe, that keeps us from falling into disorder. There is nothing more dangerous than a home without a strong leader, without a clear head to govern it. Without order, there is chaos. Without rules, there is ruin."

I had nodded, hands clasped in my lap, listening as he spoke, as he outlined the expectations that would shape my days, my thoughts, my actions.

First, there would be no questioning God's order. The Bible had already made it clear, women were to submit to their husbands, to obey, to serve with joy. That was not up for debate, not open to discussion. "We don't ask why," he said, his voice gentle but firm. "We don't second-guess what God has ordained. The moment we allow doubt to creep in, we invite rebellion. And rebellion leads to ruin."

Second, my duties were my own. The home was my domain, my responsibility, the place where my work would glorify God. It was not a task to be taken lightly. Every meal I prepared, every floor I scrubbed, every task I completed was an act of worship, an offering of service. "A well-kept home is a reflection of a well-ordered heart," he told me. "If there is disorder in the home, there is disorder in the soul."

Third, there would be no outside interference in our marriage. No gossip, no complaints, no discussions of our life beyond what was necessary. "A wife does not speak against her husband," he said, his gaze steady. "She does not seek counsel from those who would weaken her resolve. Our marriage is between us and God, not between you and the world."

I had nodded again, absorbing each rule, committing them to memory. They made sense. Of course they did. They were biblical, right, the foundation of a strong and godly household. I should have felt relief, gratitude that my husband was leading our home with such wisdom, that there was no confusion, no uncertainty. And yet, as I lay in bed that first night, staring at the ceiling, the weight of it pressed down on me in a way I hadn't anticipated. The walls of our home, the silence, the absence of anything that did not belong to him, to us, to God, it was overwhelming, consuming, absolute.

I turned onto my side, eyes tracing the shadowed patterns of the curtains, the shapes shifting in the moonlight. There was no noise from the outside world, no hum of cars, no distant laughter, no glow from a screen flickering in the darkness. There was only this house, this silence, this new life stretching endlessly before me.

And in the quiet, something inside me whispered a question I was not allowed to ask.

What if I had made a mistake?

Entry 5—
My First Lesson in Submission

It began in a way that almost seemed insignificant, a moment so small I might have forgotten it if not for the way it settled in my chest, heavy and unmoving, like a stone pressed deep beneath my ribs. I had always known there would be lessons, adjustments, small corrections as I learned how to take my place beside my husband, beneath him in the order of things. That was the way of biblical marriage, the way God had designed it. A wife was not born knowing how to be obedient, how to serve with perfect humility, how to anticipate the needs of her husband before he even spoke them. She had to be taught, guided, molded like clay in the hands of the man who had been given authority over her.

My mother had warned me that marriage was work, but she had not said it with resentment, only quiet resignation, as if stating a truth as simple as the rising and setting of the sun. *You will have to learn*, she had said. *You will have to unlearn certain things, too. A wife who cannot be corrected is a wife who invites trouble into her home.* I had nodded then, believing that I understood. Believing that because I had been raised for this, because I had spent my entire life preparing, it would come naturally. That submission would be as simple as breathing.

But standing there in the kitchen, my fingers still damp from the dishwater, my mind struggling to piece together the exact moment things had shifted, I realized how little I truly knew.

It had been something small. A misplaced dish, an unfinished task, a moment of distraction that had led me to forget to wipe down the counter after preparing lunch. I had not even noticed it, had not thought it would matter, until I felt his presence behind me, his silence heavy enough that my body tensed before he even spoke.

"You left a mess."

I turned, my hands gripping the towel I had been using to dry them, my gaze automatically dropping slightly in deference. "I—I was just about to clean it," I said quickly, feeling warmth rise to my cheeks, the sudden, sharp prick of embarrassment tightening in my stomach.

His expression did not change. "Then why is it still there?"

I opened my mouth, then closed it, my mind scrambling for an answer, an explanation that would make this moment dissolve into nothing, that would let me push past the sudden discomfort curling inside me. But there was no answer, no excuse that would suffice. He was right. The counter should have already been clean. I should not have needed to be reminded.

"I'm sorry," I murmured, my voice small, careful.

His gaze held mine for a moment longer before he nodded, stepping past me to inspect the rest of the kitchen, as if assessing my work, my ability, my commitment to the role I had promised to fulfill. "A wife must not be careless," he said. "She must not make her husband have to correct her on things she should already know."

I nodded quickly, eager to show my agreement, my willingness to learn. "I'll do better," I promised, swallowing hard, my hands tightening around the towel in my lap.

A pause. Then, he reached out, his fingers grazing my chin, tilting it upward so that my eyes met his. The touch was not harsh, not cruel, but there was something about it that made my breath catch, made my pulse quicken in a way that had nothing to do with love or tenderness. "See that you do," he said softly. "I have high expectations for you."

And then he was gone, leaving me standing there, my skin burning where he had touched me, my stomach still twisting with the weight of my own failure.

I turned back to the counter, grabbing a cloth and scrubbing away the invisible remnants of my mistake, my hands moving with a newfound sense of urgency. *This is good*, I told myself. *This is what I wanted. A husband who would guide me. A husband who would make me better.*

A good wife does not bristle under correction. A good wife does not hesitate or question. She learns. She listens. She accepts.

And I would.

Later that night, as I sat at my small writing desk, my journal open before me, I hesitated before picking up the pen. The day replayed itself in my mind, over and over again, each detail sharpening in my memory. My failure. His correction. The quiet approval in his eyes when I had accepted it without argument. That was what mattered most. That I had not resisted. That I had shown him I could be shaped.

Still, when my pen touched the paper, the words that formed beneath my fingers were not the ones I had expected.

Is this what my mother meant by "Marriage is work"?

I stared at the sentence, my lips pressing together, something unfamiliar and uneasy settling in my chest.
Then, before I could dwell on it any longer, before the thought could take root, I closed the journal and tucked it away, slipping it beneath my folded nightgowns where it would remain unseen, unread.

I turned off the light, climbed into bed beside my husband, and told myself that tomorrow, I would do better.

The next morning, I woke before the sun, slipping quietly from bed so as not to disturb him. I moved through the motions of my morning routine with a new, sharpened awareness, my steps measured, my hands deliberate in their work. The memory of yesterday clung to me, not as a wound but as a lesson, one I was determined to take to heart. A wife who needed constant correction was not yet a wife worth praising. I would make sure that I never put myself in the position to be chastised again.

As I moved through the house, I found myself watching the spaces around me differently, seeing them as he might see them. I scanned the countertops for anything out of place before I began cooking, ensuring that every surface was wiped clean before he could notice anything amiss. I double-checked the way I folded the towels, the way I set the table, the way I carried myself through the home, careful not to move too quickly or appear rushed. I paid attention to the way I held my body, the way I spoke, the way I responded when he addressed me. No more immediate apologies, no nervous explanations. Just listening, just obedience, just the quiet assurance of a wife who did not need to be reminded of her place.

He noticed.

At breakfast, he watched me more than usual, his eyes lingering as I served him, as I moved through the room with quiet efficiency. He did not immediately speak, but I could feel his approval in the way he observed me, in the slight nod he gave as I set down his coffee, in the way his posture eased just slightly, as though I had done well. That was all I needed. No grand declarations of satisfaction, no excessive praise. Just the knowledge that he saw me trying, that I had proven I could take his words and apply them without question.

"You're learning," he finally said, his voice measured, even.

Relief flooded through me. "Yes," I answered, careful to keep my voice soft but assured.

He reached for his coffee, lifting it to his lips before pausing. "Good," he said. "That is what I expect from you."

And that was the end of it. No need for anything more. I had pleased him, and that was all that mattered.

For the rest of the day, I carried that small approval with me like a quiet triumph, repeating his words in my head whenever I felt the weight of adjustment pressing down on me. I was learning. I was becoming the wife I was meant to be. This was how marriage worked, one lesson at a time, one correction at a time, until I was shaped into something worthy of his leadership.

But later that night, as I sat alone in our bedroom, the weight of the day settling over me, I felt something unexpected tug at the edges of my mind. I had done well today. I had avoided mistakes, had received no further correction, had earned his approval. So why did I feel as if I had lost something?

I stared at my journal, hesitant to open it, unwilling to see the words I had written the night before. I had thought the question was fleeting, a passing thought that would dissolve as I adjusted to my new life, but now I wasn't so sure. The words still lingered, just beneath the surface, quiet but persistent.

Is this what my mother meant by *Marriage is work*?

I hadn't known what I meant when I wrote it, not fully. But now, as I sat there in the dim light, I felt something stir beneath the thought, something I wasn't ready to name. I closed the journal without writing anything new, tucking it away as I had the night before, burying the thought along with it.

Tomorrow, I would be better. Tomorrow, there would be no need for questions.

Entry 6—
Women's Study Group

The women's study group met every Wednesday afternoon in the pastor's wife's living room, a space that smelled of lemon polish and worn Bibles, its walls adorned with framed scripture and cross-stitched reminders of a woman's role in the kingdom of God. The room was always warm, almost too warm, as if the air itself carried the weight of discipline, the quiet expectation that every woman who entered understood why she was there. It was not a social gathering. It was not a place for idle chatter or mindless fellowship. It was a space for learning, for correction, for reinforcing the order that God Himself had established since the first woman was pulled from Adam's rib.

I had been invited, no, expected, to attend as soon as I was married. "It will help you," my husband had told me. "The older women have much to teach. You'll learn what it means to be a godly wife, to carry yourself in a way that honors me." He had spoken the words as if they were a gift, as if I should be grateful that I would have the guidance of women who had already walked the path I was now on, who could teach me the lessons they had learned through years of submission and refinement. And I was grateful. At least, I told myself I was.

I arrived early, dressed modestly, my hair pinned back neatly the way I had seen the other women wear theirs. The older wives were already there, seated in a perfect circle, their hands resting on their laps, their postures poised and still. The younger wives, the ones like me who were still learning, still adjusting, sat just inside the circle, listening, watching, absorbing. There was no casual conversation, no exchange of personal thoughts or worries. This was not a space for self-expression. This was a space for instruction.

The pastor's wife, a woman with a quiet but unshakable authority, opened the meeting with prayer, her voice smooth and unwavering as she asked God to grant us the wisdom to hear His truth, the humility to accept it, and the strength to apply it in our marriages. When she finished, there was a moment of silence, a collective pause as we each bowed our heads in reverence before she spoke again, this time directing her gaze toward us, the new wives, the ones still being shaped.

"A woman's heart is deceptive," she began, her eyes scanning our faces as if to ensure we understood the weight of her words. "It is prone to selfishness, to vanity, to indulgence. It craves comfort over duty, pleasure over sacrifice, control over obedience. And that is why we must discipline it. That is why we must be vigilant."

The women around me nodded in solemn agreement, their expressions reflecting years of hearing the same truth, years of practicing the discipline she was speaking of. I felt my own head nodding along with them, though I was still grasping at the fullness of what she meant.

"Your desires," she continued, "are the devil's whisper. They lead you away from your role, away from the protection of your husband's authority. They tempt you into believing that you were made for something other than service, that your thoughts, your wants, your ambitions are as important as his. But they are not. They never have been."

I swallowed, the words settling inside me like stones dropped into deep water, their weight spreading outward in slow, rippling waves. It wasn't that I disagreed. I had been raised to understand this truth, had known for years that Eve's greatest sin had been listening to herself instead of to God. But hearing it now, spoken so plainly, so decisively, made it feel sharper, more absolute.

The pastor's wife lifted her Bible then, turning its thin pages with careful precision before reading from Titus 2:5. "To be self-controlled, pure, working at home, kind, and submissive to their own husbands, that the word of God may not be reviled."

She looked up, meeting our gazes one by one. "Self-control begins with silencing the self. A wife who allows her desires to rule her heart is a wife who invites chaos into her home. And a home in chaos is a home that dishonors her husband."

I felt my hands tighten around the fabric of my skirt, pressing it between my fingers, as if grounding myself in the physical world would help me better absorb what I was being taught. It made sense. It all made sense. And yet, as I listened, a quiet question stirred in the back of my mind, one I immediately pushed away before it could take shape.

The lesson continued, moving from scripture to practical instruction, from biblical principle to daily application. We were taught how to guard our minds against discontent, how to pray away thoughts that could lead to rebellion, how to recognize when we were slipping into selfishness and correct ourselves before our husbands needed to do it for us. A good wife, we were told, never needs to be disciplined by her husband because she has already disciplined herself. A good wife knows her place and remains in it without question.

At the end of the meeting, we were given time for reflection, for writing down the truths we had learned, the parts of ourselves we needed to correct. I took my journal from my bag, opening it to a fresh page, staring at the blank space before me. I could have written a summary of the lesson, a verse to meditate on, a note of gratitude for the wisdom I had been given. But instead, without thinking, my pen moved across the paper, forming words that felt as if they had been waiting for me to find them.

I am a rib, not a soul. I am a shadow, not a whole.

The words sat there, staring back at me, stark and unfamiliar. I read them once, then twice, my pulse quickening as I realized what I had written, as I understood that somewhere, deep inside me, a part of me was still reaching for something else, something unspoken.

I shut the journal quickly, pressing my hands over the cover as if I could lock the words inside, keep them from being seen, from being known.

The meeting ended with another prayer, another reminder that our lives were not our own, that our duty was our greatest purpose, that obedience was the highest form of love. As I stood to leave, the other women smiled at me, their eyes filled with the kind of quiet approval that told me I had done well today, that I was on the right path.

I smiled back, tucking my journal beneath my arm, my heartbeat steady and sure.

Tomorrow, I would do better. Tomorrow, I would silence the part of me that still longed to be something more.

The walk home from the women's study group felt longer than usual, though my feet moved at the same steady pace along the dirt road that led back to our house. The evening air was cooling, the sky darkening just enough that the first stars had begun to prick through the fading blue. I should have been replaying the lesson in my mind, reflecting on the wisdom I had received, preparing myself to put it into practice as soon as I stepped through the door. That was the expectation, the whole point of these meetings, to absorb, to implement, to grow into the kind of wife God intended. And yet, my thoughts were tangled around something else, something I could not quite unravel.

The words I had written in my journal still sat heavy in my mind, their shape lingering as if I had carved them into my own skin instead of the page. I had not planned to write them. They had spilled out of me, unbidden, unexamined, before I had even realized what I was thinking. I am a rib, not a soul. I am a shadow, not a whole. The words felt foreign, yet they belonged to me in a way I could not deny. Had I written them in acceptance? In defiance? I didn't know. I wasn't sure I wanted to know. All I knew was that I had snapped the journal shut the moment the ink dried, hiding the thought before it could breathe too deeply.

By the time I reached home, the lights inside glowed warmly through the windows, the house a quiet sanctuary tucked away from the rest of the world. My husband was already home, seated at the kitchen table with his Bible open in front of him. He looked up as I entered, his expression unreadable, though I could sense the way he took in my posture, my mood, the smallest details of my presence. He was always watching, always measuring.

"How was the meeting?" he asked, his voice steady, expectant.

I set my bag down, smoothing the fabric of my skirt as I moved toward the stove to check the pot of soup I had left simmering before I left. "It was good," I said carefully, keeping my voice light. "The lesson was about discipline. About guarding against selfishness."

He nodded once, as if he had already known that would be the subject. "And what did you learn?"
I hesitated only for a fraction of a second before answering. "That a wife must keep her heart in check. That our desires are the devil's whisper, pulling us away from our duties."

His gaze lingered on me for a moment longer before he closed his Bible, folding his hands together on the table. "Good," he said simply. "That is true."

I turned back to the stove, stirring the soup with slow, deliberate motions, feeling the weight of the conversation settle around us. He did not need to ask if I understood my role, he assumed it. And I did understand. I did. I had always known what was expected, what was required of me. It wasn't the lesson itself that had unsettled me. It wasn't even the pastor's wife's words, sharp as they had been. It was the way the lesson had *felt*, not like something I needed to learn, but like something I already knew too well. Like something I had been practicing since before I even had a husband to submit to.

I served him his bowl first, waiting for him to take the first bite before I sat down across from him, my hands folded in my lap. He ate in silence, and I mirrored him, chewing slowly, carefully, waiting for the moment when he would speak again. He always led the conversation in our home, determining what was worth discussing, what was worth teaching, what was worth correcting. But tonight, he remained quiet, his focus fixed on his food, and I took it as a sign that I had done well, that I had pleased him.

Still, my mind refused to quiet, even as I moved through the rest of the evening with practiced ease. I cleaned the dishes, wiped the counters, folded the towels in neat, symmetrical squares. Each action was done with purpose, with the mindfulness I had been taught to cultivate. And yet, the words still echoed in the back of my mind, soft but insistent.

I am a rib, not a soul. I am a shadow, not a whole.
Later, when we were in bed, the house wrapped in silence, I lay still beside him, my body relaxed but my mind restless. He had fallen asleep quickly, his breathing even, his presence solid and unmoving beside me. I turned my head slightly, watching him in the dim light from the window, studying the lines of his face, the quiet authority that remained even in sleep. This was my husband. The man I had been given to, the man who led me, who shaped me, who ensured that I did not stray. He was good to me. He was patient. He was strong. He was everything a husband was meant to be.

So why did I feel the strange, quiet pull of something else, something I couldn't name?

I closed my eyes, willing the thought away, pressing it down until it was nothing more than a whisper in the dark. Tomorrow, I would wake up and start again. I would prepare breakfast before he even left the bed, I would keep my posture straight, my voice gentle, my obedience unwavering. I would not fidget. I would not hesitate. I would not allow myself to stray from the path laid out before me.

Tomorrow, I would not let myself wonder if there was more than this.

Tomorrow, I would forget that I had ever asked the question at all.

Entry 7—
My First Failure as a Wife

The mistake was small, so small that in another life, another world, I might not have thought twice about it. The soup had simmered too long, the bottom of the pot catching the slightest bit of char, filling the kitchen with the faint scent of something overcooked. I had noticed it the moment I lifted the lid, the way the broth had darkened, the way the steam carried an edge of bitterness. It wasn't ruined. It wasn't inedible. It was only a little off. A little wrong.

I should have started over. I knew that the moment I hesitated, standing there with the spoon still in my hand, my mind racing through the steps I would need to take to correct the mistake. I could have dumped it, rinsed the pot, and begun again, even if it meant dinner would be late. That would have been the better option. The safer one. But I had been so careful, so diligent, so sure that I had done everything right, and the thought of wasting it, of admitting failure, of standing before him and explaining why the meal wasn't ready when it should have been, it had been enough to make me pause.

So I ladled the soup into bowls, careful to take from the top, where the flavor was still intact, where the mistake could be hidden, where I might be able to pretend it hadn't happened at all. I placed his bowl in front of him, folding my hands together as I sat across from him, waiting, watching, hoping that the meal was salvageable enough that he wouldn't notice. That I would be able to move past this without having to acknowledge it, without having to sit with the weight of my own failure.

But the moment he lifted the spoon to his lips, I knew.

He didn't say anything at first. He simply took another bite, then another, his expression unreadable, his movements controlled, as if he were giving me one last chance to correct myself, to confess before he had to address it. I should have said something then. I should have lowered my eyes and admitted it. But the words stuck in my throat, my hands tightening around the fabric of my skirt, my breath caught between the impulse to explain and the fear that the explanation would not be enough.

And then he set the spoon down.

He didn't slam it. He didn't raise his voice. He didn't even look at me. He simply exhaled, long and slow, the sound heavier than it should have been, heavier than words.

"You burned the soup."

It was not a question. It was not an accusation. It was a statement, delivered with the kind of quiet finality that left no room for argument, no room for excuses.

I swallowed hard. "I—" My voice faltered. "Yes. I'm sorry."

Silence.

He didn't move, didn't acknowledge my apology, didn't offer any sign that my words had even reached him. He only sat there, staring at the bowl, his expression unreadable, his disappointment settling over the table like a thick fog.

"I thought you knew better than this," he finally said, and it was that, more than the words themselves, more than the tone, more than the weight of his silence, that sent a sharp, sick feeling curling in my stomach.

I wanted to explain, to tell him it wasn't that bad, that I had tried to fix it, that I had been careful. But I knew better than that. Excuses were useless. Explanations were unnecessary. A wife does not justify her mistakes. A wife takes correction, learns from it, and does better next time.

So I nodded, lowering my gaze, my throat tightening as I forced out the only response that mattered. "I will."

He didn't answer.

He didn't eat.

He didn't speak another word.

The meal stretched on in silence, the sound of my own chewing suddenly unbearable, each bite turning to ash in my mouth. When he finally stood, leaving his bowl half-finished, I stayed where I was, staring at the place where his hands had rested on the table, the imprint of his touch lingering even after he was gone.

That night, as I lay beside him in bed, his back turned to me, his breathing slow and even but unmistakably distant, I felt the full weight of what had happened settle onto my chest. He had not punished me. Not in any way that could be named. There had been no anger, no raised voice, no reprimand beyond the simple acknowledgment of my failure.

But the silence was worse.

It stretched between us like an abyss, deep and impassable, a quiet void that swallowed every attempt I might have made to bridge the gap. I wanted to reach for him, to apologize again, to promise that it would never happen again. But I knew that wouldn't help. I had already said too much, already drawn attention to my own failure in a way that should not have been necessary. A good wife does not require reassurance. A good wife does not need to be soothed when she has done wrong.

So I lay still, staring at the ceiling, my body tense with the quiet knowledge that this would not pass quickly. That his silence was not a fleeting mood but a lesson, a correction of its own.

The next morning, he rose before I did, dressing without a word, leaving the room without touching me, without even looking at me. I followed soon after, moving through the house with careful precision, ensuring that everything was in place, that there was no trace of yesterday's mistake lingering in the air.

But his silence remained.

He did not acknowledge me as he left for work. He did not kiss my forehead, did not say his usual "Be good today." He simply walked out the door, and I stood there, the sound of his absence louder than anything else.

For the next two days, it continued. He spoke only when necessary, his words clipped and perfunctory, his presence in the house more like a shadow than a man. He was not cruel. He was not unkind. He simply existed beside me as if I were not there, as if I had not yet earned the right to be fully seen again.

And I understood.

This was my punishment.

Not through anger, not through discipline, but through distance.
I had failed, and until I proved that I had learned, until I corrected myself in a way that did not require further instruction, he would withhold his warmth, his attention, his presence.

That night, after he had gone to bed, I sat at my desk, my journal open before me, the words forming before I could stop them.

Marriage is work.

I stared at the sentence, at the simplicity of it, at the quiet truth in it.

Then, without thinking, I wrote again.

A wife who fails is a wife who must correct herself.

I closed the journal before I could write anything more, before my thoughts could turn to places I wasn't ready to go.

Tomorrow, I would do better.

Tomorrow, I would earn back what I had lost.

The days passed with the same cold silence, a quiet that followed me from room to room, settling into the spaces where his voice should have been. He did not touch me. He did not meet my eyes. He did not raise his voice or demand anything of me beyond what was necessary. And yet, his presence carried weight, his unspoken disappointment pressing down on me with more force than any lecture or reprimand ever could.

I knew better than to ask when it would end. That was not for me to decide. A wife does not set the terms of her own forgiveness. She waits, she learns, she corrects. And so, I moved through each day with heightened care, ensuring that everything was in its rightful place, that the meals were made perfectly, that I was anticipating his needs before he had to voice them. I set the table with precision, cooked with meticulous attention, scrubbed the floors until my hands ached. But still, the silence remained.

At night, he turned away from me in bed, his body a barrier between us. I lay awake, staring at the ceiling, the empty space between us stretching wider with each breath. I had never felt more alone, and yet, I knew this was part of the lesson. A wife who fails her husband fails God. And until I had proven myself, until I had shown that I was worthy of his affection again, this was the natural consequence.

On the fourth day, something shifted. It was small, barely noticeable, but I felt it the moment it happened. As I set his coffee down in front of him that morning, his eyes lifted, meeting mine for the first time in days. The moment was brief, fleeting, but it was enough to send a rush of relief through me, enough to tell me that my efforts had not been in vain.

I kept my expression neutral, careful not to reveal too much, not to reach for the comfort I so desperately wanted. I simply nodded, lowering my gaze in silent acknowledgment, before stepping away to continue with my morning tasks. But I carried that moment with me for the rest of the day, holding onto it like a promise, a signal that the distance between us was beginning to close.

That night, as I lay beside him, my breath shallow, my body still, I felt the bed shift slightly. A moment later, the warmth of his hand brushed against mine.

It was not an apology. It was not an invitation to speak. But it was something. A small offering. A sign that I had endured, that I had been patient, that I had proven myself.

I closed my eyes, exhaling softly, willing myself to absorb the lesson completely. I had learned what I needed to learn. I had seen what happened when I faltered, when I failed to meet expectations. And I had no intention of repeating the mistake.

The next morning, he spoke to me as if nothing had happened. The silence was gone, the balance restored, the lesson complete. I responded with quiet obedience, my voice steady, my demeanor composed. There was no need to discuss what had passed between us. It was understood.

That evening, I opened my journal, my hands steady as I turned to a fresh page. The words came easily this time, their meaning clear, their purpose undeniable.

A wife must be careful.

A wife must be watchful.

A wife must not invite correction.

I closed the journal, tucking it back beneath my folded dresses, its pages filling slowly with truths I was only beginning to understand.

Tomorrow, I would be better.

Entry 8—
A Baby?

The idea took root slowly, curling itself around my thoughts like a vine creeping up the side of a house. At first, it was just a whisper, an idle hope, something soft and distant. A baby. The word carried weight, a promise, an answer to an unspoken question. A way to set things right. A way to secure my place.

I had seen it happen with other wives in the study group. The quiet ones, the ones whose husbands seemed distant, unreadable, always measuring. They had bloomed when they became pregnant, their burdens lightened by the simple fact that they had fulfilled their highest calling. They were no longer just wives. They were mothers. And that changed everything. I had watched as their husbands softened toward them, their presence no longer something to be corrected but something to be protected. A woman with a child was no longer just a wife who needed instruction. She was the vessel of something greater, something divine.

The thought comforted me, settled inside me like a secret prayer. A baby would fix things. A baby would bring us closer. A baby would remind him why he chose me, why I was here, why I belonged to him. The silence that had stretched between us, the quiet punishments, the unspoken expectations, maybe they would disappear, maybe they would be replaced by something gentler, something warmer.

I began to notice the way the other women spoke of children, how their voices lowered when they talked about the sacred responsibility of motherhood, the pressure to conceive woven into every conversation, every lesson, every quiet moment. They asked me about it, about when we would start a family, about whether we had been blessed yet. There was no question of *if*, only *when*. A wife without children was unfinished, incomplete, a tree that had yet to bear fruit. And fruitless trees were eventually cut down.

I prayed on it at night, my hands folded tightly in my lap, whispering the words into the dark, willing God to hear me. *Let it happen. Let me be worthy. Let me be more than just a wife. Let me be a mother.*

The pressure was not spoken aloud, not by my husband, not in any direct way. But it was there, in the way he looked at me sometimes, in the way his hand lingered on my waist, assessing, expectant. It was in the way his mother asked about it whenever we visited, her smile polite but her eyes sharp. "Soon, I hope?" she had said last time, the words hanging in the air like a challenge.

I had smiled, nodding, feeling my own body betray me with its emptiness.

I started watching for signs, for any shift in my body that might mean something had changed, that something had taken root. I counted the days, felt for every ache, every moment of dizziness, every wave of nausea that might have meant an answer to my prayers. I imagined what it would feel like to tell him, to see his expression change, to hear the words *you will be a father* and know that everything between us would be different.

But the days came and went, and nothing changed.

At first, I told myself it was too soon, that these things took time, that I just had to be patient. But patience soured into something else, something tight and panicked, something that made my throat close up every time I saw another woman with her hand resting over the soft swell of her belly.

I could not fail at this.

I had already learned what failure meant, what it felt like, how it settled into the air between us, turning warmth into distance, into silence, into something I could not break.

I could not bear to disappoint him again.

The study group lessons became sharper, the words cutting in a way they never had before. "A wife's purpose is to build her husband's house," the pastor's wife reminded us, her voice even, her eyes scanning our faces, lingering on the younger wives, the ones still waiting, still trying. "To refuse him children is to refuse God's will. A barren wife is a warning, a sign that something in her spirit needs correcting."

I swallowed hard, nodding along with the others, pressing my hands into my lap until my fingers ached.

Something in her spirit needs correcting.

Was that what this was? A test? A punishment? A way for God to remind me that I still had work to do, that I had not yet learned enough, that I had not yet been stripped of whatever pride still clung to me?

I could be better. I could pray harder. I could empty myself of whatever was keeping this from happening.

That night, as I lay beside my husband, my body curled toward his, waiting for him to reach for me, to claim what was his, I felt the weight of my own longing press into me, a sharp and desperate ache.

I wanted him to need me. Not just as a wife, not just as someone to warm his bed and serve his meals, but as something irreplaceable, something he could not turn away from, something more.

A child would bind us together in a way nothing else could.

A child would make me indispensable.

A child would mean I had done my duty, that I had proven myself, that I was worthy.

But the months stretched on, and my stomach remained flat, my hands empty.

I stopped writing in my journal.

There was nothing to say. Nothing I wanted to see written in ink, nothing I wanted to stare back at me in the quiet of the night.

I avoided the other women when I could, their gazes too knowing, their questions too pointed. I forced smiles, nodded when they spoke of their growing families, listened as they reassured one another that more children would come, that God always blessed a faithful wife.

I wanted to believe them.

I wanted to believe that faithfulness was enough.
But I had learned that obedience was no guarantee of kindness.

And I was running out of time.

Entry 9—
The Women Who Vanish

It started as a whisper, nothing more than a shift in the air, a glance exchanged between two women at the study group, the kind of thing that would have gone unnoticed if I hadn't already learned to listen for what was left unsaid. It wasn't an announcement, not something spoken plainly, but a name that had been erased before I even realized it was missing.

Her name was Miriam. She lived just a few houses down, a woman I had seen at church every Sunday, seated beside her husband, her hands always folded neatly in her lap. She was quiet, reserved, the kind of woman who never drew attention to herself, who seemed to understand her place with a certainty I envied. She had two children, both small, their faces round and cherubic, the kind of children people cooed over, the kind that made other women nod approvingly and say, *God has blessed her.*

And yet, she was gone.

At first, I thought maybe she was sick. Maybe she had fallen into some kind of quiet illness, the kind that kept a woman in bed while the world outside moved on without her. But then I noticed that her husband was still at church, alone, seated in the same pew where she should have been, his expression calm, untroubled, as if nothing had changed.

No one asked where she was.

No one whispered about when she might return.

And that was when I knew.

I had seen it before, though I had not understood it then. Women who disappeared without warning, their names slipping from the lips of the congregation, their absence never acknowledged beyond a carefully worded prayer request that hinted at vague transgressions. They were not mourned. They were not missed. They were simply *gone*, and the world moved forward as if they had never been there at all.

It was not my place to ask, but the question gnawed at me anyway. I had not known Miriam well, but I had known her *enough*, enough to recognize that whatever had happened to her was not something she had chosen for herself.

I watched the other women carefully, searching for some sign that they felt it too, that they had noticed the way her name had been erased, the way the church had already folded over the space she had once occupied. But if they had, they did not let it show. Their faces were impassive, their smiles as soft and serene as ever.

The pastor's wife addressed it once, briefly, as if checking off an item on a list, as if making sure the lesson was understood.

"She struggled with rebellion," she said simply, her voice smooth, careful, the words balanced between warning and dismissal. "And in the end, she refused correction."

No one asked what that meant.

No one needed to.

A rebellious wife was a danger to herself, to her husband, to her children, to the entire order of God's plan. A rebellious wife was a rot that could spread if left unchecked, a disease that had to be removed before it could infect the rest of the flock.

I lowered my eyes, staring down at my hands, my fingers curling against my skirt, pressing into the fabric as if grounding myself there, as if reminding myself that *I was not like her.*

I had not been tested, not in the way she had. I had been corrected, yes, had been shaped and disciplined, but I had never *resisted.* I had never pushed back. I had never given my husband reason to doubt my submission.

Had I?

That night, as I lay beside him in the quiet of our bedroom, his breathing steady beside me, my mind refused to settle. The thought of her, of Miriam, of whatever had happened to her, pressed into me like a weight, something heavy and cold, something I could not shake.

I tried to picture her, tried to remember the last time I had seen her, the last time our eyes had met across the study group, across the pews at church. Had she known? Had she seen it coming? Had she realized that her days were numbered, that she was already being erased before she had even left? Or had she woken up one morning believing that everything was the same, only to find that she was wrong?

I turned onto my side, staring at the dark outline of my husband beside me, his body relaxed, unconcerned, as if nothing had changed, as if nothing could touch him. I envied that certainty. I envied the way he moved through the world without fear, without doubt, without the quiet, creeping worry that one wrong step, one misplaced thought, could unravel everything.

I wanted to wake him up, to ask if he had noticed, to ask if he *cared.* But I already knew the answer. Miriam had been erased, and there was no room for grief in something that had already been decided.

Instead, I slipped from bed, moving carefully so as not to wake him, crossing the room to where I kept my journal tucked beneath my folded clothes. I opened it, the pages familiar beneath my fingers, the ink from my last entry still sharp and dark against the paper.

I should not have written it. I should not have let my thoughts escape in a way that could be seen, that could be read. A wife who fails is a wife who must correct herself. I stared at the words, my pulse quickening, the weight of them suddenly heavier than before. I reached for my pen, my hand steady as I wrote beneath them, my letters small, careful, a quiet promise to myself. I must never become rebellious. I stared at the words for a long time, my breath coming shallow and slow, the truth of them settling deep inside me.

I could not afford to be careless. I could not afford to be noticed. I could not afford to be erased.

I shut the journal, slipping it back beneath my clothes, pressing it down as if I could bury the words themselves, as if I could lock them away where no one, *not even myself*, could find them again.

Tomorrow, I would do better.

Tomorrow, I would be the kind of wife no one had to correct.

Tomorrow, I would make sure that my name was never one they whispered.

Entry 10—
The Community Watch

I had always known that the women in our community looked after one another. It was something spoken about with quiet reverence, an unspoken expectation that wove itself into every interaction, every conversation. *We hold each other accountable.* That was the phrase they used, always laced with a certain righteousness, a reminder that discipline was an act of love, that correction was not cruelty but salvation.

At first, I had thought it was nothing more than gentle reminders, quiet nudges when a wife needed guidance. I had imagined older women leaning in close, whispering warnings about immodest dress, about the dangers of idle gossip, about ensuring their homes remained places of order and devotion. It had not occurred to me that watching meant *watching*, that there were eyes on me at all times, that every movement, every word, every action was being weighed, recorded, stored away for later discussion.

It was not just the elders who did the watching. It was all of them.

I realized it first when I noticed how quickly they spoke of Miriam, the woman who had vanished. It was always in passing, in careful, measured words, but the message was clear, she had been watched, her failings noted, her rebellion detected long before she was gone. And now that she was gone, her absence served as a warning, a reminder that those who did not submit fully, who did not embrace their role without question, would be *dealt with.*

The fear settled into my bones, a quiet, humming awareness that stayed with me as I moved through my days. I found myself second-guessing everything, every glance, every conversation. Had I lingered too long at the market speaking to another wife? Had I hesitated before answering a question at the study group? Had I looked too tired, too restless, too distant?

A wife who fails is a wife who must correct herself.

I repeated the words like a prayer, forcing them into my mind, into my body, into my very being.

And yet, even my obedience would not make me invisible.

It was during Sunday service that I saw the full weight of the Community Watch for the first time.

The woman's name was Ruth. I had never spoken to her beyond polite greetings, though I had seen her before, seated beside her husband, her hands always folded neatly in her lap, her eyes never straying too far from the floor. She had two children, both boys, young enough to squirm in the pews before their father's firm hand stilled them. There was nothing unusual about her, nothing that made her stand out. And perhaps that was why I did not understand what was happening at first, why it took me a moment too long to register the shift in the congregation as she was called forward.

She rose slowly, her movements stiff, reluctant.

Her husband did not look at her.

The pastor stood at the pulpit, waiting, his Bible open in his hands, but he was not reading from it. He was watching her.

When she reached the front, she stood motionless for a moment before slowly lowering herself to her knees.

It was then that the murmurs started, quiet voices shifting through the room like a breeze slipping through the cracks of a sealed house. I could not make out the words, but the tone was clear, judgment, confirmation, the final recognition of something already decided.

I felt my stomach tighten.

The pastor did not have to ask why she was there. The accusation had already been made, the proof already delivered.

"Confess," he said simply.

Her hands clenched into fists against the fabric of her skirt. She hesitated. It was a mistake. The silence stretched, thick, suffocating. I could feel the weight of it pressing against my ribs, pressing against *her*, against all of us.

Finally, she exhaled, and when she spoke, her voice was hoarse, her words thin and fragile.

"I—" She swallowed. "I read something I shouldn't have."

There it was. A collective murmur rippled through the congregation, approval from some, disappointment from others.

The pastor tilted his head slightly, his expression unmoved. "What did you read?"

She closed her eyes, as if the words themselves might break her, as if saying them aloud would seal her fate.

"A book."

The room stilled. Not just *a book. A secular book.* The words were not spoken, but they did not need to be. I felt my breath catch.

It was a foolish mistake, one that should have been avoided. A wife does not fill her mind with distractions, with falsehoods, with ideas that do not serve her purpose. Reading was permitted, of course, but only the *right* reading. Scripture. Devotional texts. Approved works on biblical womanhood, on modesty, on submission. Anything beyond that was a temptation, a door left open for doubt to creep in.

She had been seen.

She had been reported.

And now, she was here.

The pastor let the silence stretch a moment longer before speaking again. "You understand what you have done?"

She nodded.

"What happens when a wife fills her mind with ungodly things?"

Her voice wavered. "She becomes discontent."

"And what happens to a discontent wife?"

She lowered her head further. "She disrupts the order of her home."

The pastor exhaled, a long, measured breath. "And you understand why you are here?"

"Yes," she whispered.

"To be corrected."

She nodded.

A long pause, then— "Who saw you?"

My breath stilled. The question was not meant for her alone. It was meant for all of us. To remind us that we were being watched. That we were all watching each other. She did not answer right away. But she didn't have to. Whoever had seen her, whoever had spoken, whoever had delivered her to this moment, they had done their duty. And that was what was expected.

The pastor closed his Bible with a quiet thud. "This will not happen again."

It was not a question. She nodded.

The silence hung heavy for another long, unbearable moment before she was finally dismissed, allowed to rise and return to her seat, her face pale, her shoulders shaking just enough for those closest to her to see.

Her husband did not look at her. And I did not dare look at her either.

When the service ended, I walked home in silence, my feet steady, my steps careful, my thoughts circling themselves into tight knots. I had never asked myself before what would happen if I faltered.

But now, I knew.
I sat at my desk that night, staring at the blank page of my journal, my hand hovering over the paper, uncertain.

The words came slowly, deliberate.

A wife must not question.

A wife must not stray.

A wife must never forget that she is being watched.

I underlined the last sentence twice before closing the journal and placing it beneath my folded dresses, pressing it down as if I could hide the weight of what I had written.

Tomorrow, I would be better.

Tomorrow, I would make sure that there was nothing, *nothing*, to see.

Entry 11— My Husband's Authority

It began so subtly I almost didn't notice. At first, it felt like guidance, like the steady hand of a husband ensuring that his wife walked the right path, stayed within the boundaries of righteousness. It was a kindness, I told myself, a comfort to be led, to be cared for so thoroughly that I did not need to make decisions for myself. The burden of choice was lifted from me, and wasn't that a blessing? Wasn't that what God intended?

My dresses were too short.

I had thought them modest, their hems brushing my ankles, their necklines high, but he frowned when he saw me wearing them, his gaze sharp with disapproval. "A wife should not draw attention to herself," he said, and when I looked down, I saw what he saw, the fabric too fitted, the way it moved with me instead of concealing me. The next day, my wardrobe changed. My skirts grew longer, my sleeves looser, the fabric heavier. I dressed for anonymity, for invisibility, for quiet obedience. And when he nodded in approval, something inside me exhaled, as if I had passed a test I had not known I was taking.

My food was too indulgent.

I had always loved sweet things, the soft, warm comfort of honey drizzled over bread, the occasional square of dark chocolate after dinner. But indulgence, he reminded me, was a form of selfishness. A wife does not eat for pleasure. A wife eats for sustenance, for strength, for the ability to serve. He took my plate one evening, examined its contents with careful scrutiny, and removed half of what I had given myself. "You don't need this much," he said, his tone even, unyielding. "You should not take more than you require." From then on, I ate what he decided I needed. No more. No less.

My sleep belonged to him.

A wife does not dictate when she rests. A wife does not decide when the day is done. She sleeps when he is finished with her, wakes before he does so that the home is already in order before his feet touch the ground. I learned this quickly, trained my body to anticipate his movements, to adjust without question. When he sat beside me in bed, his fingers curling around my wrist, I did not pull away. When he told me to stay awake, to sit with him, to read scripture aloud even when my eyes burned with exhaustion, I did. And when he told me to sleep, I closed my eyes, whether I was tired or not.

It was easier that way.

Obedience became second nature, an instinct ingrained so deeply that I did not question it, did not resist, until one evening, I did.

I had been feeling ill all day, my head thick with a dull ache, my stomach unsettled, my limbs sluggish. I had moved through my tasks as best I could, but by nightfall, my body was screaming for rest. I was in bed when he entered the room, my eyes already closing, my breathing slowing into something dangerously close to defiance.

He stood at the edge of the bed, watching me.

"You're not asleep yet," he said, but it was not a question.

I forced myself upright, my movements slow, careful. "I'm not feeling well," I admitted, my voice barely above a whisper.

His expression did not change. "You should have told me."

I nodded, waiting, hoping that he would understand, that he would allow this small thing, this moment of weakness.

But then he reached for me, his fingers gripping my chin, tilting my face up toward his. His touch was not cruel, not punishing, but it held something sharp, something unmovable.

"You do not decide when you rest," he said, his voice low, calm, final. "I do."

I swallowed, my pulse fluttering against his grip. "I know," I murmured, forcing the words out through the tightness in my throat.

His eyes held mine for a long moment before he released me, his hand falling away as he exhaled, shaking his head slightly. "You forget yourself," he said, almost to himself, as if I had disappointed him in a way he had not expected. Then, more firmly, "You are my property. Do you understand?"

The words landed between us like a weight, heavy and cold, pressing down on my chest.

I nodded.

"I need to hear you say it," he said, his voice softer now, coaxing.

I closed my eyes, inhaled slowly, steadied myself. "I understand."

And I did.

I understood that my body was not my own. That my time, my choices, my rest, my hunger, my comfort, none of it belonged to me. I understood that my existence was not separate from his, that I had been given to him, not as a partner, not as an equal, but as something owned, something possessed, something shaped by his hands and his words.

I understood that obedience was not just expected, but owed.

I understood that the moment I hesitated, the moment I allowed myself to believe I had any authority over myself, I had already failed.

And I could not afford to fail.

The next day, I corrected myself.

I asked him to approve what I wore before I left the bedroom.

I took the portion of food he set in front of me without question.

I did not sit until he told me I could sit. I did not speak unless he had addressed me. I did not close my eyes until I was given permission to sleep.

And he noticed.

At dinner, his gaze lingered on me a fraction longer than usual, his nod of approval subtle but unmistakable. When I poured his coffee, his fingers brushed over mine, a silent acknowledgment that I had learned. That I had been shaped, once again, into something more acceptable. More worthy.

That night, when I lay beside him, he pulled me close, his breath warm against my temple. "Good girl," he murmured, his voice filled with something like satisfaction.

I felt the tension leave my body, the relief washing over me like a blessing, like grace.

I had pleased him.

I had done what was expected.

I had made myself small enough to fit within the boundaries of his authority.

Tomorrow, I would do it again.

The next morning, I rose before him. The house was quiet, still wrapped in the heavy darkness before dawn, but I did not hesitate. My body moved before my mind had fully woken, my hands already reaching for the fabric of my dress, my fingers fastening the buttons with careful precision. I checked myself in the mirror, smoothing out the fabric, ensuring that I was covered properly, modestly, in a way that would be pleasing to him. My reflection stared back at me, expressionless, expectant. I adjusted the hem one last time before stepping out of the room.

The kitchen was cold, the floors unforgiving beneath my bare feet, but I ignored it. The water boiled, the coffee brewed, the bread toasted to the exact shade he preferred. I arranged his plate carefully, making sure everything was as it should be, making sure there was nothing to correct. By the time he entered the room, I was already in place, my hands folded neatly in front of me, my eyes lowered just enough to show deference but not enough to appear ashamed.
He sat without a word, reaching for his coffee first, taking a slow sip before glancing down at his plate. His expression remained unreadable, his silence stretching long enough that my pulse quickened, waiting for his reaction, waiting for confirmation that I had done well.

Then, finally, a nod.

"You're learning," he said simply.

The relief was instant, flooding through me like warmth after too long in the cold. I had done well. I had corrected my mistake. I had proven that I understood.

I took my place at the table only when he gestured for me to do so, careful to eat slowly, to mirror his pace, to take only what I had been given. I chewed deliberately, methodically, focusing on the weight of the food in my mouth, on the way it settled in my stomach. I no longer ate for pleasure. I no longer reached for more than what was required.

When breakfast was finished, I cleared his plate first, rinsing it before mine, ensuring that his needs had been met before tending to my own. He left the table without another word, but the lack of correction was as good as praise. I had done well.

The rest of the day passed in careful repetition, each task performed with quiet precision, each movement controlled. I moved through the house with purpose, my body conditioned to its rhythm, my hands steady as they scrubbed, as they folded, as they arranged. There was something soothing about it, something almost comforting in the predictability, in the certainty that if I did everything exactly right, if I gave him no reason to find fault, I could exist without fear. I did not need to think. I did not need to decide. I only needed to obey.

It was easier this way.

That night, as I lay beside him, my body still and waiting, I did not resist when he reached for me. I did not hesitate when he took what was his. I closed my eyes, my breath even, my body compliant. A wife does not refuse her husband. A wife does not withhold. A wife gives. When he was finished, he turned onto his side, exhaling in quiet satisfaction, his breathing slowing as sleep took him. I remained awake, staring at the ceiling, my limbs heavy, my mind hollow.

This was love.

This was marriage.

This was obedience.

I repeated the words silently, letting them settle inside me, letting them take root.

A wife does not resist.

A wife does not question.

A wife belongs to her husband.

I would not forget again.

Tomorrow, I would be better.

Entry 12—
The Sermon on Obedience

The church was full that Sunday, every pew occupied, every woman seated beside her husband, hands folded in their laps, heads bowed in reverence. The air was thick with the scent of old hymnals, polished wood, and the slow-burning candles that flickered at the altar, their flames unwavering even in the stillness. I sat where I always did, beside my husband, my posture perfect, my dress neat, my breath measured to match the rhythm of his. It was an expectation, an unspoken rule that had been embedded in me long before I was a wife. A woman does not fidget. A woman does not draw attention to herself. A woman listens.

The pastor stepped up to the pulpit, his Bible open, his expression calm but heavy with purpose. The sermon had not yet begun, but already, I could feel the weight of it pressing into the space around us, settling over the women like an unseen hand guiding their heads lower in submission.

"Today," he said, his voice steady, certain, filling the vastness of the sanctuary with ease, "we speak on obedience."

A pause. A quiet murmur of approval rippling through the men. A few nods from the older women, their faces serene, their mouths curved in knowing smiles.

He turned the page, running a hand over the fragile paper as though the weight of the words required reverence even before they were spoken. "Ephesians 5:22," he read, his tone unchanging. "Wives, submit to your husbands as to the Lord. For the husband is the head of the wife as Christ is the head of the church."

I did not move. I did not shift. I did not even breathe too deeply. The verse was familiar, one I had heard more times than I could count, a scripture so ingrained in me that it was no longer something I questioned but something I carried inside me like a second heartbeat.

The pastor looked up, his gaze sweeping over the congregation, pausing, just for a fraction of a second, on the wives seated in the front row.

"A wife's duty," he continued, his voice taking on a new edge, "is to honor her husband. To serve him. To suffer for him, as Christ suffered for the church. A woman who submits to her husband submits to God. A woman who resists her husband resists God's order."

A shift in the room. A tightening in my chest. I could feel my husband beside me, his presence a steady, immovable force, his breathing even, unconcerned.

"A wife does not question," the pastor said, his words slow, deliberate. "A wife does not resist. A wife does not claim ownership over her own body, her own will, her own desires. To suffer for your husband is to suffer for Christ."

I heard the faint, nearly imperceptible sound of fabric shifting as the older women nodded. Their approval was soft but solid, a quiet agreement that reinforced everything that had been said before, everything that had already been etched into our bones.

The pastor closed the Bible, though he did not step away from the pulpit. His hands rested on either side of it, his gaze heavy with expectation.
"There are those among us who struggle," he continued, his voice losing none of its steadiness. "Those who resist the order God has placed upon them. Those who, in their hearts, still hold themselves separate from their husbands."

A pause. No names were spoken, but the accusation was clear.

A rebellious wife was an open wound, a sickness that could spread if left unchecked. I could feel the way the congregation stilled, the way every woman sat just a little straighter, the way the quiet breathing of the men remained unchanged.

"We cannot allow sin to take root in our homes," the pastor said, his voice rising just slightly, enough to press the weight of his words deeper. "A wife must be purified through obedience. She must suffer joyfully, knowing that through her sacrifice, she honors God."

The words were meant to comfort, but they did not. I swallowed, my hands tightening in my lap. The sermon continued, but I had already stopped listening. I did not need to hear the rest. I already knew what it would be.

A wife belongs to her husband. A wife obeys without question. A wife does not resist. To suffer is to serve. To serve is to love. To love is to endure.

By the time the service ended, I felt the weight of the lesson settle inside me, deep and unshakable. I would not forget.

The church emptied slowly, as it always did, the congregation moving in quiet murmurs, the men speaking in low voices, their hands firm on the backs of their wives, guiding them toward the doors, toward the vehicles, toward home. I moved with my husband, my steps careful, my head slightly bowed, the echoes of the sermon still filling my ears, my chest, my throat.

The air outside was heavy, thick with the last traces of summer's heat, but I did not lift my eyes to the sky, did not let myself feel the sun on my skin. I kept my gaze ahead, my movements controlled. The other wives moved the same way, their silence a kind of shared understanding, their expressions calm, unreadable.

The pastor's words were still with us.

To suffer for your husband is to suffer for Christ.

A wife's duty is to honor her husband, to serve him, to endure for him, to sacrifice.

A wife must be purified through obedience.

The words had not been new, but they had felt heavier today, as if they had been spoken directly to me, as if they had settled inside my ribs like something permanent, something that could not be undone.

We reached the vehicle, and my husband helped me inside, his touch light but firm, his fingers pressing just hard enough against my wrist to remind me that he was the one guiding me, the one leading me. I sat where I always sat, my hands folded neatly in my lap, my dress smoothed over my knees, my breathing measured.

He did not speak until we were halfway home.

"That was a good sermon," he said finally, his voice steady, assured, expectant.

"Yes," I said softly, because it was the only acceptable answer. He turned his head slightly, looking at me, assessing. "It is good to be reminded of these things."
I nodded, though the motion felt stiff, unnatural. There was a long pause, the quiet stretching between us, filling the small space, thick and heavy.

Then, almost too casually, he said, "You understand why suffering is necessary?"

I forced my hands to remain still in my lap, forced my voice to remain steady. "Yes."

Another pause.

"You don't sound sure."

I swallowed, my throat dry. "I am."

His gaze lingered a moment longer before he turned back toward the road, his hands resting on his knees, relaxed, content. "Good," he said simply. "A wife who understands her place is a wife who will be blessed."

I nodded again, though he was no longer looking at me, though the conversation had already ended.

When we reached the house, I stepped from the vehicle first, moving quickly to the door, opening it before he had to reach for it, ensuring that the home was prepared for his return, that there was nothing out of place, nothing to correct.

Inside, I moved through the motions of my duties with quiet precision, my mind still turning over the words spoken in the church, the way the older women had nodded, the way the pastor's voice had carried so easily through the sanctuary, filling every corner, leaving no room for doubt, no room for questioning. To suffer for your husband is to suffer for Christ.

I had always known this, had been taught this since girlhood, but today, the words had felt different. I had felt them in my bones, in the way my chest tightened when they were spoken, in the way I had barely breathed as I listened, as if my body already knew what was coming, as if it was bracing itself for something inevitable.

The older wives had nodded. The men had remained still, unmoved, expectant. The younger wives had sat quietly, absorbing, accepting, understanding. A wife must endure. A wife must obey. A wife must love through suffering.

I poured his coffee exactly the way he liked it, careful not to let the liquid rise too high in the cup, careful to place it in front of him without a sound, careful to move away just as he reached for it, ensuring that I was not in his way, ensuring that there was nothing to displease him.

He took a sip, nodding slightly, his approval quiet but present. I exhaled. The rest of the evening passed without incident. I prepared dinner, set the table, ate exactly the portion he had given me, did not speak unless he spoke first, ensured that everything remained as it should be.

When it was time for bed, I undressed in silence, folding my dress neatly before slipping beneath the covers, waiting, listening. He did not touch me that night. He did not have to. I had already learned the lesson. I had already understood.

Suffering is necessary. Obedience is love. Submission is worship.

I closed my eyes and prayed that I would be better tomorrow.

Entry 13—
My Thoughts Are a Sin

It started as a flicker, barely a thought, something so small I might have ignored it if I had not learned to fear even the whispers in my own mind. I had been kneeling, hands clasped, eyes closed, lips moving in silent prayer, when it came. A quiet shift, a ripple in the stillness. A question.

I could not even name it, not at first, not as the words of my prayer carried on, not as I forced my breath to stay even, not as I tried to drown it beneath scripture, beneath obedience, beneath everything I had been taught to hold as truth. But it was there, moving beneath my thoughts like something waiting to be unearthed. A doubt. A hesitation. A shadow against the certainty I had built my life upon.

I pressed my fingers tighter together, my nails digging into my palms, a silent reprimand, a warning to myself. *God forgive me. Doubt is rebellion.*

The words came instantly, automatic, written into the very structure of my being. Doubt was the first step toward destruction. Doubt had been Eve's sin before she reached for the fruit, before she doomed all of creation with her hunger for knowledge. Doubt was a wife's first betrayal, the crack that spread before the foundation crumbled. A wife does not doubt. A wife does not question. A wife does not think in ways that lead her down dark paths.

And yet, I had.

I did not know where it had come from, only that it had settled into me before I could stop it, before I could cast it away. Had it been during the sermon, when the pastor's voice had rung out through the church, calling us to obedience, to suffering, to joyful submission? Had it been when I had watched the older wives nod, their faces calm, their agreement so complete it no longer seemed to require thought? Had it been when my husband's fingers tightened around my wrist, the weight of his authority pressing into my skin in the way I had been taught to welcome, to cherish?

Or had it been there all along, waiting beneath the surface, waiting for the moment when I would falter just long enough for it to slip through?

I should have repented immediately. I should have thrown myself at God's mercy, should have prayed until the doubt had been burned from me completely. But I had hesitated, if only for a moment, and that, too, was sin.

I exhaled slowly, forcing my shoulders to relax, forcing my body to remain still, controlled. There could be no sign of unrest, no sign that anything within me had shifted, no sign that I had allowed even the smallest crack in my devotion. A wife who questions is a wife who has already failed.

I lowered my forehead to the ground, my breath hot against the floor, the pressure of the position familiar, comforting in its absoluteness. I was small here, nothing more than a servant at the feet of my master, a vessel waiting to be filled with righteousness. I was emptying myself of myself. I was making space for obedience, for submission, for faith.

God forgive me. God cleanse me. God make me new again.

I remained there for a long time, long enough for my knees to ache, long enough for my breath to slow, long enough for the silence to stretch so wide it swallowed everything else.
When I finally rose, I moved carefully, deliberately, as if I could step out of the sin that had tried to take root inside me, as if I could leave it there on the floor, forgotten, abandoned.

I would not let it happen again.

I moved through the house with renewed purpose, tending to my tasks with more care than usual, ensuring that every movement was precise, that every duty was completed without error. I scrubbed the floors until my hands ached, pressed the iron so firmly into the fabric that the heat burned against my fingers, folded the laundry with the kind of attention that made the corners sharp, the stacks perfect. I did not stop. I did not allow my mind to wander. A wife should be too busy for idle thoughts.

By the time my husband returned, the house was immaculate, and I was steady, my expression composed, my posture flawless.

He sat at the table, his eyes scanning the room, the quiet hum of approval in his demeanor the only sign I needed that I had done well. I served him dinner without a word, keeping my hands careful, my movements precise.

When he finally spoke, it was not to offer praise, but to remind me.

"A wife does not need to think beyond her duty," he said, his voice even, expectant.

I nodded, lowering my gaze. "Yes."

He studied me for a moment longer before returning to his meal.

I had been seen.

I had been measured.

And I had passed.

That night, when I sat alone at my desk, the house wrapped in silence, I opened my journal, my fingers moving before I could stop them, before I could remind myself that there was nothing to confess beyond my own weakness.

God forgive me. Doubt is rebellion.

I stared at the words, my breath shallow, my fingers tightening around the pen.

I could not allow this to happen again.

I could not afford to question, to falter, to let the seed of doubt take root.

I closed the journal, tucking it away, burying it beneath the folded fabric of my dresses, pressing it down as if I could bury the thoughts themselves, as if I could crush them beneath the weight of my own obedience.

Tomorrow, I would be better.

Tomorrow, I would not allow my mind to betray me.

Entry 14—
The Day I Wanted to Leave

It happened in the dead of night. At first, no one knew she was gone. No one suspected, because no one ever did. A woman who belonged to a man did not simply *disappear.* A woman who had taken vows, who had been led properly, who had been shaped into obedience, did not *leave.* But she had.

I didn't know her well. I had seen her in church, had watched her kneel during prayer, had listened to her voice rise in unison with the other wives during hymns. She had been quiet. Diligent. She had never stood out. That, I think, was why it was so shocking. It wasn't the loud ones, the resistant ones, the ones who still needed shaping, who ran. It was always the ones who had appeared *settled.* The ones who had seemed to understand. The ones who had done everything right.

I had heard the story secondhand, passed in hushed voices, carried like a warning through the study group, though no one dared to ask too many questions. I didn't even know how she had done it, how far she had gotten, if she had planned it for weeks or months, if she had laid awake every night, waiting, breathing, willing herself to take the first step. But she had tried. That was the part that mattered.

She had not gotten far. A woman alone is easy to catch. They found her before sunrise. And now, she was gone. Not dead, or at least, no one had said that. But she was gone in the way Miriam had been gone, in the way the other women had vanished, their names spoken once and then never again, their absence nothing more than a quiet space where a body used to sit. They did not bring her back to church. She did not return home. No one asked where she was. No one asked what had been done to her. We already knew.

The punishment for rebellion was never spoken of directly, but we had all seen what happened when a woman *failed.* When a woman lost her place, when she refused to be molded, when she forgot that her body was not her own.

Correction could be silent. A prolonged absence, a quiet removal, the erasure of a name, the closing of a door. Correction could be public. The slow, deliberate stripping of dignity, the forced confession, the tears that came too easily and meant nothing at all. Correction could be brutal.

No one asked which had been done to her. No one asked *because they were afraid to know.* That was how I knew she had been erased properly, completely. No one spoke her name. No one said *she should have known better* or *she had always been difficult* or *it was bound to happen sooner or later.* No one even *pretended* to pity her.

She was not an example. She was not a lesson. She was nothing now. And the morning after I learned of her vanishing, I woke up with a single thought pressing against my ribs, swelling inside my lungs, forming so thick and heavy in my throat that I thought I might choke on it.

I want to leave.

It wasn't even a *want*, not exactly. Not a decision, not something fully formed. It was a realization, something that had been buried deep within me for longer than I cared to admit, something that had been waiting, waiting, waiting for me to see it.
I want to leave.

The thought alone was a sin. It was rebellion. It was dangerous, as dangerous as running, as dangerous as disappearing into the night, as dangerous as stepping one foot out of line. I was not supposed to think like this. I was not supposed to *want.* I had been trained, conditioned, reshaped into something that did not question, that did not *consider* another life beyond this one.

And yet, I did.

I moved through the day with the weight of it pressing down on me, thick and unbearable, clinging to my skin like a fever I could not sweat out. I was careful not to let it show, careful to keep my expression blank, my voice light, my posture perfect. I *knew* I was being watched.

A wife is always being watched.

The other women, the older wives, the ones who nodded at every sermon, the ones who whispered warnings and reminders about what a wife should and should not be, they were always looking for the cracks. They were always searching for the signs of something that needed to be corrected before it could spread.

I smiled when I was supposed to smile. I nodded when I was supposed to nod. I did not hesitate. I did not falter. But the thought remained.

I want to leave.

I had never dared to imagine *how.* Had never dared to consider *where I would go, what would happen, what I would become* if I made it beyond the boundaries of this life. I had only ever seen what happened to the ones who failed.

I had only ever seen what happened to the ones who *tried and lost.* And yet, the thought would not leave me.

That night, I sat at my desk, my journal open before me, my hands trembling as I gripped the pen. I should not have written anything. I should have let the thought die in my chest, should have buried it beneath obedience, beneath scripture, beneath the silent, steady acceptance of my place. But my hand moved before I could stop it.

She is gone, and no one speaks her name.

I exhaled sharply, the words staring back at me like an accusation. I should not have written them. I should not have let them take shape, should not have allowed them to exist beyond the space of my own mind.

I nearly crossed them out. Nearly ripped the page from the journal, burned it, let the ink dissolve into nothing, let the words disappear just as she had disappeared. But I didn't. Instead, I sat there, my breath shallow, my pulse pounding in my ears, my body rigid with the unbearable, inescapable weight of a truth I could no longer deny.

I want to leave.

I closed the journal slowly, carefully, pressing my hands over the cover, as if I could silence the thought itself, as if I could push it back into the place it had come from.

I could not run. I could not leave. I had seen what happened to the ones who did. But the thought had already taken root. And no matter how deeply I buried it, I knew—

It would never go away.

The thought did not leave me, no matter how much I prayed, no matter how much I worked, no matter how much I pressed my hands together until my knuckles ached and whispered, *God, forgive me, God, cleanse me, God, take this from me.* It clung to me like something rotten, something growing beneath my skin, something that had always been there but had never before been strong enough to rise. Now it had, and no matter how much I told myself that I was not like *her*, that I would never be like *her*, that I would never run, never betray my vows, never allow my mind to be filled with such rebellion, I knew I was lying.

I was already betraying. I was already running, even if my feet had not yet moved.

I thought of her constantly. The nameless woman who had tried. The one who had left in the night, believing she could slip past the eyes that never stopped watching, past the husbands who held the keys, past the walls built from obedience and punishment, past the god she had been told was always looking, always waiting to strike. I imagined her gathering her skirts in her fists, imagined the way she must have forced herself to move quickly, quietly, even though every part of her must have been screaming that she would not make it, that she would be caught, that she would be dragged back.

I wondered what she had been thinking when she was found. If she had known, in those final moments before they reached her, that she had lost. If she had felt it settle into her chest, the knowing, the sick understanding that she would not make it, that she had never really stood a chance. I wondered what she had been told as she was taken, if the men had spoken to her with disappointment or fury, if she had been given time to explain herself before they decided what would be done to her.

I thought of what must have happened next, though I could not let my mind stay there for too long.

Had she been brought home, to be corrected behind closed doors, her screams swallowed by thick walls and the silence of a congregation that had already erased her?

Had she been sent somewhere else, somewhere where she could no longer infect the rest of us with the dangerous idea that *leaving* was possible?

Had she simply disappeared, her punishment something no one would ever speak of, something we were only meant to understand in the way we understood everything else, without question, without protest, without allowing our minds to ask too much?

I would never know.

But I understood now that it had been a mistake to believe that no one ever wanted to leave. That every wife I saw had been born into this life without hesitation, without resentment, without a quiet, gnawing feeling deep inside them that something was *wrong*.

No one spoke of her, but I knew, *I knew*, that there had been others before her. There would be others after. I would be one of them. The thought settled inside me, and I could not unthink it. I would not run tonight. I would not run tomorrow. I did not know when. I only knew that the day would come. And that when it did, I would not be caught.

That night, I stood at the kitchen sink long after my husband had gone to bed, my hands submerged in water that had gone cold, my breath steady but shallow. The house was silent, the air still, the only sound the faint rustling of the wind against the windows.

I could leave now. I could go, just as she had gone, slip into the night, into the empty streets, into the darkness beyond. I could take nothing, leave no sign, force myself to move quickly, force myself not to hesitate. But I did not. Because I knew better. Because I knew what happened to the ones who ran without thinking, without planning, without ensuring that the moment they took their first step, they *would not be caught.*

So I stayed.

I dried my hands.

I turned off the light.

I walked to my room, to my husband, to my place beside him.

I lay still in the darkness, my body quiet, my breath even, my eyes open, staring at the ceiling.

I was not ready yet. But I would be. And when I was—

No one would find me.

Entry 15—
The Women's Punishment Room

I had heard of the room before, but only in whispers, only in the careful, measured way women spoke when they wanted to pretend they were not speaking at all. A place never acknowledged, never named directly, just referenced in half-finished thoughts, in stories that never quite reached their endings. I had seen the way the older wives stiffened when it was mentioned, the way their faces smoothed over with something unreadable, something cold, something distant. I had seen the way their hands tightened around the edges of their skirts, the way their eyes dropped just slightly, as if they were remembering something they had already spent years trying to forget.

I had noticed the way the younger wives listened carefully but never asked questions, never pressed too hard, never let their curiosity get the best of them. Because a woman who asked too much, who wanted to know more than she should, was a woman who might one day end up behind that locked door herself.

I had told myself I would never see it. That I would never need to. That if I was careful, if I obeyed, if I smothered every stray thought before it could take root, I would never have to know what waited in that room. But then, one day, I did.

It was not supposed to happen.

I had been cleaning, my hands raw from scrubbing the stone floor of the main hall, my knees aching from the hours spent kneeling, the cold sinking into my bones until I could barely feel them at all. I had been careful that day, as I always was, ensuring that everything was done properly, that there was nothing to be corrected, nothing to be questioned. My body was sore, my mind blank, the repetition of my duties numbing in a way that felt almost comforting.

And then I heard it.

The sound was faint at first, barely distinguishable from the quiet murmur of voices further down the hall, from the movement of feet across the floor, from the distant hum of the world continuing on as it always did. But as I turned the corner, as I stepped into the corridor that led to the far end of the house, I heard it again. A muffled cry. A sound that was not meant to be heard at all.

I stopped.

For a long moment, I only stood there, my breath shallow, my heart slow and heavy in my chest, my hands still damp from the soapy water I had left behind in the bucket. I told myself to move. To turn around. To continue with my tasks and pretend I had not heard anything at all.

But then I heard the voice.

It was familiar.

It was *hers*.

Anna.

My stomach clenched, a sharp, sick feeling twisting deep inside me. Anna, who sat beside me in the women's study group. Anna, who had smiled at me just days ago, who had squeezed my hand in quiet reassurance when I had faltered during prayer, when I had lost my place in the scripture I had been reciting. Anna, who had been the first to notice when I had withdrawn, when I had begun to slip into my own thoughts more than I should. She had not pressed me, had not pried, but I had *felt* her watching. I had seen the flicker of something like worry in her eyes, something that she had never said aloud, something that had never needed to be spoken.

And now she was behind that door.

I should have walked away.

I should have left before someone saw me, before someone realized I had been standing there too long, before I had done something that could not be undone.

But I didn't.

I stepped closer.

The door was thick, heavy wood reinforced with iron, a door that did not belong in a house of worship, a door that did not belong in a home at all. It was a door meant to *keep things in*. A door meant to ensure that no one left until they were *allowed* to leave.

Another muffled cry.

I pressed my hand against the wood, my fingers trembling, my breath catching in my throat.

I did not call her name.

I did not speak at all.

I only listened.
The sounds were soft, but they were unmistakable. Sobs, choked and desperate, the kind of crying that a woman does when she knows no one will come for her, when she knows she is alone, when she knows that whatever is happening behind that door will not stop until *they* decide it will.

I clenched my jaw, my nails digging into the palm of my hand so hard that I thought they might break the skin. I knew better than to knock. I knew better than to let myself be seen lingering too long in a place where I should not be.

I forced my hands to my sides.

I forced my feet to move.

I forced myself to walk away.

That night, I sat at my desk, my journal open, my pen hovering above the page, my breath shaking.

She was there. Behind the door. And I left her there.

I swallowed, my throat tight, the weight of it pressing against my ribs.

I had not saved her.

I could not save her.

Because there was no saving anyone.

Because Anna would leave that room only when they decided she was ready.

Because Anna would return to her place in the study group, beside me, with the rest of the women, with the same quiet obedience she had always had, with the same nods of approval at the sermons, with the same hands folded neatly in her lap.

And she would *never* speak of it.

Just like no one had ever spoken of the women who had disappeared.

Just like no one had ever spoken of the punishments we *knew* were happening, but never dared to name.

She was there. And I left her.

The words stared back at me, cold and unforgiving.

I closed the journal, pressing my hands over the cover, as if I could crush the truth of it, as if I could force it back into the place where all unspoken things went to die.

I climbed into bed beside my husband, curling into myself, my body rigid with the knowledge that no amount of obedience would ever make me safe.

Because it did not matter how well I obeyed.

It did not matter how much I submitted, how much I prayed, how much I erased myself in an attempt to fit into the space they had carved out for me.

The door would always be there.

And one day, it might be me behind it.

The door did not exist. That was the understanding, the unspoken rule that held the weight of a command. No one looked in its direction. No one asked questions. No one acknowledged what happened behind it, or what became of the women who spent their time locked away within its walls. It was as if it had never been built, as if the house of God, the sanctum of our righteous community, had no need for such a thing. And yet, it stood there, solid and unmovable, as much a part of our lives as the prayers we spoke each morning, as the obedience that shaped every step we took. I told myself I had not seen it, that I had not heard what I had heard, that Anna had not been inside, that I had not stood outside, listening to her sobs while my hands trembled against the wood. But I had. I had heard everything. And worse, I had left her there. I had turned away, my breath caught between my teeth, my steps careful and measured, returning to my duties as if nothing had changed. That was what was expected. That was what was required.

Anna returned three days later, walking into the study group as if nothing had happened. Her hair was braided neatly down her back, her dress pressed and clean, her hands folded carefully in her lap. I watched her, waiting for some sign that she was different, waiting for some flicker in her expression that would betray what had been done to her behind that door. But she gave nothing away. Her eyes never lifted from the floor, her voice never wavered when she repeated the scripture, her posture remained perfect, without hesitation. But I knew. I could *feel* it. The tension in her shoulders, the way her fingers twitched slightly against the fabric of her skirt, the way she never once shifted in her seat, as if the simple act of moving would unravel her completely.

No one acknowledged her absence.

No one asked where she had been.

No one said her name in any way that would suggest she had not been sitting among us just days before.

I wanted to speak to her, to pull her aside after the lesson, to whisper, *I know.* I wanted to reach for her hand the way she had once reached for mine when she had sensed my hesitation, when she had noticed my quiet withdraw into myself. But I did not. Because I knew better. Because I understood now that to acknowledge what had happened to her, to *recognize* it, was to invite the same fate upon myself. She was not Anna anymore. She was someone else now, someone reshaped by the same hands that had molded all of us, that had carved us into obedient, silent wives.

I kept my eyes forward.

I nodded at the lesson.

I recited the scripture.

I pretended.

That night, as I stood at the sink scrubbing dishes, my hands moving on their own, my mind circling the same thought over and over, I heard my husband enter the kitchen behind me. I did not turn, but I felt the weight of his presence, the way he watched me, the way he measured everything about me in the smallest of gestures, the way I held myself, the way I breathed, the way my fingers gripped the ceramic edges of the plates.

"You've been quiet," he said, and it was not a question.

I swallowed, forcing my body to remain still. "I have nothing to say."

The silence stretched behind me, heavy and unbroken.

Then, a step closer. His hand settled against my lower back, light but firm, pressing just enough to remind me that he was there, that I belonged to him, that my silence, my thoughts, my very being were not my own. "That's good," he murmured. "A wife who talks too much invites trouble."

I closed my eyes, forcing the air slowly from my lungs, my hands tightening around the last dish in the sink. "Yes," I said, my voice even. "I understand."

His fingers lingered for a moment longer before he pulled away, satisfied.

I waited until I heard his footsteps retreat, until I was alone again, the kitchen still and quiet except for the sound of water dripping from the faucet.

I dried my hands, wiped the counters clean, ensured everything was in its proper place before turning toward the small desk in the corner of the room. My journal sat beneath my folded linens, hidden but never too far from reach. I retrieved it carefully, my fingers trembling only slightly as I opened it, the blank page staring back at me like a challenge.

I should not have written anything.

I should have let the thoughts die in my chest, let them dissolve into the empty silence I had created within myself. But I couldn't. The words were already there, forming too quickly for me to stop them, spilling onto the page before I could remind myself that they were dangerous, that they would destroy me if they were ever found.

Anna was in the room. I heard her. I left her. And now she is back, and no one speaks of it. She is different now. She is not the same. She is not Anna anymore.

I pressed the pen harder against the paper, my breath shallow, my pulse loud in my ears.

What did they do to her?

I didn't know. I would never know. But I had seen what she had become, and that was enough.
I closed the journal quickly, my chest tight, my throat burning, my hands unsteady as I shoved it back beneath my clothes, pressing it down as if I could bury the words, as if I could make them disappear before they could betray me.

I stood there for a long moment, staring at nothing, my mind hollow, my body numb.

I had done what I was supposed to do. I had walked away. I had kept my silence. I had obeyed. And still, it was not enough. Because the door existed. Because Anna had walked through it, and she had come back as someone else. Because now, I knew—

One day, it would be me.

Entry 16—
The Nightmares Begin

The dreams started quietly, creeping into the edges of my sleep like shadows slipping beneath a locked door. At first, they were nothing more than flickers, brief flashes of something I could not quite hold onto. A sound. A feeling. A weight pressing into my chest. I would wake with my heart pounding, my breath caught between my teeth, my body stiff with something I could not name. But the images never lasted. They vanished the moment I opened my eyes, dissolving into the darkness of the room, leaving behind nothing but the dull ache of fear curling in my stomach.

I told myself it was nothing. A side effect of exhaustion, of overwork, of the strain that came with trying so hard, every single day, to be perfect. I prayed before bed, pressing my hands together so tightly my fingers ached, whispering the words with more urgency than I ever had before. *God, cleanse me. God, protect me. God, do not let these thoughts take hold.* I fell asleep with scripture on my lips, my body curled into itself, trying to make myself small enough that the nightmares would pass over me entirely.

But they didn't.

They grew worse.

The first time I dreamed of running, I woke up gasping, my fingers twisted in the sheets, my skin slick with sweat. The memory of it was still sharp, clear in a way no other dream had ever been. I had been barefoot, my feet sinking into the dirt, my lungs burning, my legs trembling beneath me. The world around me had been dark, the air thick with the sound of my own breath, my own pulse pounding so loudly I could barely hear anything else. But I knew they were behind me. I could feel them. The weight of them, the inevitability of their hands reaching for me, the certainty that no matter how fast I ran, no matter how hard I tried, I would not make it. And I hadn't.

The moment their fingers closed around my wrist, I had woken with a sharp, strangled gasp, the feeling of their grip still lingering, as real as the bed beneath me, as real as the breath that shuddered through my chest.

I sat up slowly, my body stiff, my skin cold despite the heat in the room. My husband slept beside me, his breathing deep, steady, unbothered. I turned my head slightly, watching the slow rise and fall of his chest, listening to the sound of his breath filling the space between us. I had never envied him before. But in that moment, I did.

He did not dream like this. He did not wake in terror, his body still caught between two worlds, his mind still convinced that the hands reaching for him were real. He had no reason to.

I swallowed hard, pressing my fingers into my lap, trying to steady myself. The dream was not real. I was here. I was *safe.* There was no reason to be afraid. And yet. I could still feel the dirt beneath my feet. The sharp sting of twigs scratching at my legs as I ran. The burn in my lungs as I gasped for air, knowing, even in the dream, that it was useless. That I would never outrun them. I clenched my jaw, forcing myself to lie back down, to press my head against the pillow, to slow my breath, to find the steady rhythm of my husband's breathing and match it. I did not sleep again that night.

The next day, I was careful. More careful than I had been before. I measured my steps, my movements, the tilt of my head when I spoke, the way I folded my hands in my lap, the way I set my plate in front of my husband, ensuring that there was nothing, *nothing*, to correct. A wife must be diligent. A wife must not let her mind wander. A wife must be perfect.

But even as I moved through the day with precision, even as I nodded at the study group, even as I murmured agreement to the pastor's wife, I could *feel* it. The dream clinging to me, wrapping itself around my ribs, tightening every time I let my guard slip. That night, I dreamed of running again. This time, I made it farther.

I did not know where I was going. The road ahead of me stretched endlessly, disappearing into the horizon, no landmarks, no signs, nothing to tell me if I was headed toward freedom or straight into the hands of those who would drag me back. But I *ran.* My legs burned with the effort, my breath came in sharp, ragged gasps, my skin slick with sweat and dirt and desperation.

And then, just as I thought, *Maybe, maybe this time.*

I heard them. Footsteps behind me. The rustling of branches breaking. A voice, low and steady. "Stop."

I tried to move faster. My feet slipped, my hands caught the ground, my knees buckled, but I forced myself back up, forced my body forward, *forward, forward*, because I knew what would happen if I didn't. And then—

A hand on my shoulder. A weight pulling me back. The ground rising up to meet me.

I woke with a cry, my throat raw, my breath coming too fast, too shallow, my heart hammering so hard I thought it might crack my ribs. My hands flew to my arms, my shoulders, my legs, searching for bruises that were not there, for dirt that did not stain my skin, for fingers that had not truly touched me.

My husband shifted beside me, exhaling sharply before turning onto his side, his back to me. He had not woken. He had not *heard* me.

I pressed my hands against my mouth, trying to quiet the uneven sound of my breath, trying to steady myself, trying to convince myself that it had only been a dream.

But the fear was real.

The certainty was real.

No matter how many times I ran, I would never get away.

I climbed out of bed slowly, my limbs weak, my stomach twisting itself into knots. The house was silent, the only sound the faint creaking of the wooden floor beneath my bare feet. I moved carefully, my breath shallow, my pulse still unsteady. I didn't know where I was going. I only knew I could not stay in that bed, with that dream still pressing against my skin, with the weight of it making it impossible to breathe.

The kitchen was dark, the moonlight barely enough to illuminate the edges of the table, the outline of the cabinets, the faint glint of the knife resting by the sink. I stared at it for a long moment, my body frozen, my thoughts suspended somewhere between the dream and the waking world.

I could leave. I could walk out the door right now. I could run. And yet. I knew how the story ended. I had already seen it.

I forced myself to turn away, to step back, to move toward the desk in the corner of the room where my journal was hidden beneath my folded clothes. My hands were still trembling as I opened it, as I let the pen press into the paper, as I let the words spill from my fingers without hesitation, without control, without *thought.*

I ran. They caught me. I will always run. And they will always catch me.

I stared at the words, my breath slow, my hands unsteady. I knew what they meant. I knew what I was admitting. I knew that no matter how much I obeyed, no matter how much I submitted, no matter how much I tried to erase myself.

I wanted to leave.

And one day, I would.

I closed the journal, pressing my hands over the cover as if I could silence the words inside, as if I could make them disappear before they destroyed me. But the truth was already there. And now, I could never take it back.

Entry 17—
My Husband Finds My Hidden Journal

The nightmares bled into my waking hours, slipping through the thin barrier between sleep and consciousness, taking hold of me even in the brightest moments of the day. I would be kneeling in prayer, hands folded, lips moving in quiet submission, and suddenly I could feel the dirt beneath my feet, the cold air burning my lungs, the weight of unseen hands reaching for me. I would be scrubbing the floors, my fingers raw, the soap burning against the open cracks in my skin, and in my mind, I would hear footsteps closing in, voices murmuring just behind me, warning me that I would never escape. I would be listening to the pastor's wife read from scripture, nodding when expected, murmuring agreement when required, and all I could hear was the sound of my own breath in the dark, the echo of my own pounding footsteps as I ran toward nowhere.

I was no longer certain where the dream ended and the truth began.

Sleep no longer belonged to me. Each night, I lay still beside my husband, waiting for the darkness to take me, knowing it would not be rest that found me but terror. And yet, as soon as the first threads of exhaustion wove their way through my body, I would slip back into that endless, hopeless run. No matter how fast I moved, the hands always caught me. No matter how far I went, the door always waited. No matter how much I begged, no matter how much I fought, I always woke with the feeling of fingers wrapped around my wrists, of a body dragging me back, of a voice murmuring in my ear, *It is time for correction.*

I told myself I was safe. I told myself it was only fear, only exhaustion, only the weakness of a mind that had strayed too far from obedience. But I knew better.

Because now, when I woke in the dark, breathless, trembling, heart pounding, I knew that my time was running out. I had not run yet, but the fear was already inside me. And fear was its own kind of rebellion.

I moved through the days in careful silence, ensuring that my hands never shook when I poured my husband's coffee, that my breath never hitched when he touched me, that my steps remained steady and measured, my voice never wavering. But I was not perfect. I could feel my control slipping, fraying at the edges, unraveling like a hem worn too thin.

One morning, as I stood at the kitchen sink, my hands submerged in the cold water, scrubbing a plate that was already clean, I felt his eyes on me. I did not turn. I did not speak. The air between us tightened, stretched taut like a rope about to snap.

"You're distracted," he said finally, his voice even, unreadable.

I swallowed, pressing my hands flat against the ceramic dish beneath the water. "I'm tired."

The lie tasted bitter on my tongue. A pause. A long breath. Then—

"You are thinking too much."

I closed my eyes. A wife should not think beyond her duties. A wife should not fill her mind with questions. A wife should not dream.

"I'm sorry," I murmured.

His hand settled on the back of my neck, not gentle, not cruel, just firm. Just a reminder.

"Don't let it happen again."

I nodded, the movement small, careful. The pressure of his hand lingered a moment longer before he pulled away, leaving me standing there, my breath caught somewhere between my chest and my throat. I did not move until I heard his footsteps retreating down the hall. Then, slowly, I exhaled.

That night, I did not write in my journal. Not because I had nothing to say, but because I was afraid of what the words might reveal. I had already written too much. Too many thoughts. Too many truths. I had left pieces of myself scattered across the pages, pieces that could be found, that could betray me, that could become the weight that dragged me back when I finally ran. I told myself I would destroy it. That I would burn it, bury it, rid myself of it before it was too late.

But I didn't. Because I was not ready to let go of the only proof I had that I was still *me*. Because even if I could not run yet, I needed something to hold onto, something that whispered *you are real* when everything around me was trying to erase me.

I hid it beneath my folded clothes, deeper this time, pressing it down beneath the weight of fabric, my hands shaking as I tucked the edges between the layers. Then, I forced myself to sleep. And, as always, I ran. The path was different this time. The trees gave way to open fields, the sky stretching endless and empty above me, no landmarks, no direction, just the wide, aching nothingness of a world that did not care if I escaped or if I was dragged back. I ran until my legs burned, until my breath came sharp and ragged, until the weight of my own fear threatened to crush me.

And then—

The hands. The weight. The ground rushing up to meet me. But this time, I did not wake. This time, I felt the grip tighten. Felt the voices murmuring. Felt the world shift around me, closing in, swallowing me whole.

And then, from the dark

A new voice. Not one of the faceless men. Not my husband. Not the pastor. Not the voices I had always feared. A woman's voice. Soft. Familiar.

Whispering.

Run.

I woke with a sharp gasp, my body trembling, my pulse hammering so loudly I could barely hear the silence around me.

My hands flew to my arms, my legs, searching for the bruises that my dream-self had earned, for the dirt that should have stained my skin.

Nothing. Only sweat. Only shaking fingers. Only the lingering echo of that voice. *Run.*

I sat there in the dark, breathless, listening to the sound of my husband's even breathing beside me. And, for the first time since the nightmares began, I realized, I wasn't the one warning myself. I wasn't the one whispering in my own ear. *Someone else had been in that dream.* Someone who had run before. Someone who had lost. And someone who wanted me to *go before it was too late.* I did not sleep again that night.

I lay in the dark, staring at the ceiling, waiting for the first traces of morning light, waiting for the moment when I could move again, waiting for the moment when I would finally stop pretending. I had already made my decision. I just hadn't admitted it yet. But I would.

And soon.

I spent the next day in a haze, my body moving through the routine of my duties while my mind replayed the voice over and over. *Run.* It was not a command. It was not a plea. It was something deeper, something that had wrapped itself around my ribs and lodged itself inside me. I was no longer certain whether the voice had come from a dream or from something else entirely. I only knew that it had spoken the truth.

I was running out of time.

I had spent too long convincing myself that if I obeyed well enough, if I erased my thoughts, my doubts, my fears, I would be safe. But safety had never been real. It had only been the illusion of security, a fragile thing that could be shattered with a single misstep, a single mistake, a single moment of being *seen* too clearly.

And I had been seen.

I could feel it in the way my husband watched me, his gaze heavier than usual, measuring, waiting, searching for something beneath my silence. I had been too careful these past weeks, too restrained. Perhaps he sensed it. The way my hands no longer trembled when he touched me. The way I moved without fear, without anticipation of correction. The way I had become still, not with obedience, but with something else entirely. Resolve.

I had decided. And somehow, he knew.

That evening, as I prepared his supper, my movements remained steady, controlled. I did not rush. I did not hesitate. But my stomach clenched as I felt him enter the room, his presence a force that pressed against me like the weight of a stone tied to my ankles.

I turned, careful not to meet his eyes too directly. He did not sit at the table. Instead, he stood near the doorway, watching.

"You've been different," he said.

The words sent a shiver down my spine, though I did not let it show.

I kept my voice even. "I don't know what you mean."

His head tilted slightly. "Don't you?"

I swallowed. The walls of the house seemed to close in, pressing too tightly around me.

"You wouldn't keep secrets from me, would you?"

I felt my pulse jump. He knew. I did not ask what he meant. I did not allow my breath to change, my body to betray me. But it was too late. He stepped forward. Slowly. Deliberately.

"You see, I was looking for a shirt today," he said, his voice almost casual. "In our room. In the wardrobe."

My stomach twisted.

"And as I was searching, I found something that doesn't belong."

The air in the room stilled. I forced myself to move, turning back toward the table, reaching for the plate I had just finished preparing.

"You must be mistaken."

The lie felt heavy on my tongue, thick with desperation. A sharp sound cut through the silence. Something hitting the table. I did not have to turn to know what it was. My journal. My breath caught. I could feel him watching me, waiting. I did not move.

"You've been writing things," he said, his voice quieter now, more dangerous. "Things a wife should not think. Things a wife should *not* say. Things that make me wonder if you have forgotten your place."

I closed my eyes, my nails pressing into my palms. I had known this would happen. I had known the risk. And yet, I had not prepared myself for *this*. I turned, slowly, my face composed, my hands steady. "It's only thoughts."

His jaw tightened.

"Thoughts," he repeated.

I nodded. "I am not perfect."

It was the only thing I could say. The only thing that might save me.

For a moment, he did not move. Then, just as I thought he might speak again, he reached for the journal, flipping it open with slow, deliberate movements. His eyes skimmed the pages. I forced myself to remain still. Then, he read.

I want to leave.

My heart pounded so hard I thought I might be sick. He let the words hang in the air between us, thick, suffocating. His fingers pressed against the edge of the book, his grip tightening. Then, in one quick, violent motion, he tore the page from its spine. My breath hitched. Another page. Then another. He ripped them without looking, without hesitation, his movements methodical, unhurried, deliberate.

"You have been corrupted," he murmured. "Your mind is sick."

I said nothing. He reached for another page. Another. Another. The sound of paper tearing filled the room, each rip slicing through the air like a knife against flesh.

"You need correction."

The words were final. Absolute. I knew what was coming before he moved. I had seen it before. I had *felt* it before. But this time, it was different. This time, it was *worse.*

He reached for me. And I did not fight. I did not flinch. I did not beg.

Because this time, I understood something I had not understood before. He thought he was breaking me. He thought he was *fixing* me. But he had already lost. Because I was not afraid anymore. Because I had already made my decision. Because I would not be here much longer. He could punish me. He could tear me apart. But he could not keep me. Not forever. Not anymore.

And as the first blow landed, I did not cry. I only closed my eyes, inhaled slowly, and thought, *soon.*

Entry 18—
The First Attempt

The night I tried to leave, the air was thick with silence. The kind of silence that stretched across the walls of the house, settling into its corners, pressing against my skin like something waiting to catch me. The house had always been quiet, filled with careful movements, hushed voices, obedience carved into every breath. But tonight, it was different. Tonight, the silence held weight, expectation. As if it knew. As if it had been waiting for me to try.

I had been planning it for weeks, maybe longer. I had mapped out the steps in my mind, rehearsing them in the hours before sleep, refining them in the moments when my hands were occupied but my thoughts were not. I had studied the routine of the house, the way my husband moved through the night, the way his breathing slowed in deep sleep, the way the wooden floors creaked under weight but not when I stepped lightly, carefully, deliberately. I had tested the back door, its lock, its handle, the way it could be eased open just enough to slip through without a sound.

I had prepared. And yet, I hesitated.

I lay in bed, staring at the ceiling, my pulse pounding against my ribs, my breath shallow. My body ached from the last punishment, my skin still tender where his hands had reminded me of my place, but none of it mattered anymore. I had made my decision. There was no turning back. If I did not leave tonight, I never would.

I moved slowly, peeling the blanket away inch by inch, careful not to let the fabric whisper against my skin. My husband's breathing was deep, steady. I turned my head slightly, just enough to see the shape of him in the dark, his body unmoving, his face slack with sleep. He would not wake easily. I had learned that over the years, the way he could sleep through storms, through the crying of a baby in the next room, through the quiet shuffle of my feet when I moved through the house in the earliest hours of the morning. He would not wake unless I made a mistake.

I slid my feet to the floor, feeling the cool wood against my soles, pressing my toes down just enough to keep my weight even. I rose, moving carefully, one step at a time, each breath measured. The room stretched long before me, every shadow sharper, every sound amplified. The door was only a few feet away. I just had to reach it.

I stepped forward. The wood groaned beneath me. I froze. His breath did not change. He did not move. I exhaled slowly, continuing toward the door, pressing my fingers against the knob and twisting it with a deliberate slowness, feeling the latch slide free. I stepped into the hallway. It was darker here, the air thicker, the weight of the house pressing down as if it, too, understood what I was trying to do. The back door was at the end of the hall, just beyond the kitchen. If I moved quickly but carefully, I could be outside in less than a minute.

My steps were silent, each one placed with precision. I did not think of what came after, where I would go, how I would survive. I could not afford to think that far ahead yet. I only needed to be *out*. I reached the kitchen, my hand stretching toward the door. And then, I felt it.

The shift in the air. The presence behind me. Before I could move, before I could think, fingers wrapped around my wrist, tight, unyielding, pulling me back. My breath left me in a sharp gasp as my body twisted, my free hand flying up instinctively before I caught myself. I knew better than to struggle. I knew better than to fight. But for a second, just a second, I wanted to. The grip on my wrist tightened as I turned to face him. My husband. His eyes were unreadable in the dark, his expression calm, but his fingers dug into my skin, his body still as he studied me. There was no shock in his face. No anger. Only quiet certainty.

"You were going somewhere," he said.

It was not a question.

I swallowed, my throat dry. "I—"

There was no use in lying. He had caught me.

His fingers flexed, pressing harder against my wrist. "You were trying to leave."

It was not anger in his voice. It was something worse. Disappointment. Like I had failed a test I hadn't realized I was taking. Like he had expected better of me. I didn't answer. I didn't need to. His grip shifted, moving from my wrist to my upper arm, steering me away from the door, back into the house, back toward the hallway, back toward what I already knew was waiting. The punishment. But this time, it would be different. This time, I had done more than hesitate. I had done more than question. This time, I had *acted*. And for that, there would be no simple discipline. No quiet correction. This time, I would be taken to the pastor.

The thought made my stomach tighten, my breath turn sharp. I had seen it before, the way women were brought to him when their husbands could not correct them alone. The way they disappeared into his study, the way they came out quieter, more obedient, their bodies stiff with something they never spoke of. I knew what was coming. And I could do nothing to stop it.
My husband did not speak as he led me through the house, his grip steady, his movements careful. He was not angry. That was what terrified me the most. He did not throw me to the floor. He did not strike me. He did not yell. He simply moved with the quiet certainty of a man who knew he had already won.

The walk to the pastor's house was not long. The night air was cool against my skin, but my body burned, my pulse fast and unsteady, my legs weak beneath me. I did not struggle. I did not pull away. I had no choice.

We reached the house, its windows dark except for the study, where a dim glow flickered behind the heavy curtains. My husband did not knock. He did not need to. The door opened before we reached it. The pastor stood there, waiting. He was an older man, his frame thin but unbent, his hands soft, untouched by labor. His eyes settled on me, then flicked to my husband.

"She tried to leave," my husband said. The words were quiet, spoken without emotion.

The pastor exhaled through his nose, stepping aside. "Bring her in."

I did not resist as my husband guided me inside. The door closed behind us with a soft, final click.

The study was lined with bookshelves, the smell of old pages and candle wax thick in the air. There was a chair in the center of the room, its wood polished, its design simple.

A chair meant for *correction*.

I had never sat in it before. I had never thought I would.
My husband moved me toward it, pressing me down gently. My body obeyed before my mind could protest, my back straight, my hands settling in my lap.

The pastor lowered himself into the chair across from me, his gaze steady, assessing.

"This is very serious," he said.

I nodded, though I did not trust myself to speak.

"You have been given a place of honor," he continued, his voice calm. "A husband who provides for you, who loves you, who guides you toward righteousness. And yet you have chosen rebellion."

I felt my throat tighten, my hands pressing harder against my lap.

"I have seen this before," the pastor continued. "A wife who believes she knows better than the Lord. A wife who thinks she can outrun her duty."

He leaned forward slightly.

"You cannot."

His voice was still soft, but there was steel beneath it.

I swallowed, my breath shaking. "I was—"

The pastor held up a hand, silencing me.

"You will learn," he said simply.

A pause.

Then, he turned to my husband.
"Leave her here."

The words sent a shudder through me. My husband hesitated, just for a moment. Then, he nodded. He did not look at me as he stepped back. He did not say anything as he walked toward the door. The door closed behind him. And I was alone. Alone with the pastor. Alone in the house where women went when they had been given one last chance.

The pastor sat back in his chair, watching me, his expression unreadable. Then, he smiled. And I knew. I would not leave this house the same as I had entered it. I might not leave at all.

The door closed behind my husband with a finality that sent a tremor through my body. I sat perfectly still in the chair, my hands folded tightly in my lap, my pulse hammering against my ribs. The pastor did not speak right away. He simply watched me, his fingers steepled beneath his chin, the flickering candlelight casting shadows across his lined face.

The room felt smaller than it should have. The walls, lined with books of scripture and theology, seemed to close in, pressing against me from all sides. I had been in this house before, in the gathering room where the women sat in quiet circles, nodding as the pastor's wife instructed us in obedience. I had walked these halls, my head bowed, listening as the men spoke of divine authority, of a wife's duty to submit, to serve, to suffer joyfully. But I had never been here, *here*, in this room where only the disobedient were brought.

The chair beneath me was hard, polished smooth by the weight of those who had sat here before me. I thought of Anna. I thought of the way she had returned from this house, her voice softer, her presence smaller, her obedience unquestioning. I thought of the way no one had spoken of it afterward, the way no one had dared to ask what had been done to her, how she had been *fixed*.

Now it was my turn.

The pastor sighed, tilting his head slightly as if considering where to begin. "You have put your husband in a difficult position," he said finally, his voice calm, almost kind. "Do you understand that?"

I nodded, my breath shallow.

"Speak," he instructed.

"Yes," I whispered.

He smiled, though there was no warmth in it. "Good."

He leaned back in his chair, the wood creaking beneath his weight. "I have known your husband for many years. He is a righteous man. A man of patience and wisdom. He has guided you well." His eyes darkened, his fingers tapping against the arm of the chair. "And yet, you have chosen to rebel."

I swallowed, my throat dry. "I—"

He held up a hand, silencing me.

"A wife who seeks to leave her husband seeks to leave God," he said. "And a wife who leaves God is lost."

His words were measured, spoken with the certainty of a man who had never been questioned, never been defied. I lowered my gaze, my hands tightening in my lap to keep them from shaking.

"You have allowed your mind to wander," he continued. "You have entertained dangerous thoughts. And now, you have acted on them." He shook his head, disappointed. "This is not a small sin. This is a sickness of the soul."

I felt my breath catch, a sharp, tight thing that I struggled to keep steady.

"Tell me," he said, his voice gentle, coaxing. "What made you believe you could survive without your husband?"

I hesitated, knowing that whatever I said would be used against me.

"I don't know," I murmured.

His eyes narrowed. "A lie."

I flinched.

He sighed again, shaking his head. "I do not enjoy this part of my work," he said, and for a moment, he almost sounded regretful. "But I have seen women like you before. Women who let doubt take root. Women who allow themselves to be tempted by the lies of the world. Do you know what happens to those women?"

I forced myself to shake my head.

"They are destroyed," he said simply. "They are consumed by their own selfishness, their own wickedness. They become useless to God, useless to their husbands. And when they leave, they find nothing waiting for them. No love. No protection. No salvation." He leaned forward, his gaze pressing into me. "Is that what you want?"

"No," I whispered.

His eyes flickered with approval. "Good. Then we will begin."

I forced myself to remain still as he rose from his chair, moving to a wooden cabinet in the corner of the room. He opened it carefully, his fingers tracing over its contents. I could not see what was inside, but I could hear the soft rustling of fabric, the faint clink of metal.

"I have found that different women require different methods," he said, as if discussing something as ordinary as gardening. "Some women need only words. A reminder of their place. Others need… more."

He turned back to me, something coiled in his expression, something patient. "Tell me, child. Which do you believe you need?"

I did not answer. It did not matter what I said. I already knew what was coming.

He selected something from the cabinet and returned to his chair, settling it onto his lap. A leather strap. Worn. Folded neatly in half.

I kept my eyes on the floor.

"I do this because I love you," he said.

I did not respond.

"Your husband has given you to me for correction," he continued. "And you will leave this room whole again, obedient again. Do you understand?"

I nodded.

"Speak."

"Yes."

The strap snapped against my skin before I could prepare for it, the pain sharp, immediate, burning through the thin fabric of my dress. My body lurched forward, my breath leaving me in a strangled gasp, but I did not cry out. I clenched my teeth, forcing the sound back into my throat.

He sighed. "You must *accept* this, child. You must *welcome* it."

Another strike. Harder this time. My fingers dug into my lap, my vision blurring. A wife must suffer. A wife must endure. A wife must love through pain. A wife must *learn*.

The third strike sent a white-hot flash of pain through my spine, my breath catching, my chest heaving. He paused, watching me, waiting.

"Say it," he said.

I did not speak.

The strap cracked against my skin again.

"Say it."

I clenched my jaw, shaking, my breath shallow. "I will obey."

A pause.

Then, a smile. "Good girl."

The strap was set aside. The lesson had been learned. I sat there, trembling, my body stiff, my breathing slow and careful. He watched me for a moment longer, then stood, adjusting the cuffs of his sleeves.

"You will remain here tonight," he said. "For prayer."
My stomach turned. I knew what that meant. I wanted to run. But I had already tried that once.

Instead, I bowed my head. "Yes."

The door opened. My husband stepped inside, his expression unreadable.

"She is ready," the pastor said.

My husband nodded. And then he turned to me. The strap had been easy. What came next would be worse. I had failed. But I had survived. And if I could survive this, I could survive *anything*. Even running again.

Entry 19—
The Escape Plan

The house felt different after that night. Every shadow stretched longer, every sound rang sharper, every breath I took carried the weight of something fragile, something on the verge of breaking. My body still ached, my skin still burned in places that would take weeks to heal, but that was not what haunted me. It was the *knowing.*

I had felt it before, creeping at the edges of my thoughts, whispering in the space between my ribs. But now, it was fully formed. Solid. Unshakable.

I will not survive another lesson.

That night in the pastor's house had changed something inside me. Not in the way they intended. Not in the way they believed suffering would shape a woman into submission, break her into something easier to hold, something pliable and obedient. I was quieter, yes. I was careful, yes. But it was not fear that kept me in line. It was calculation.

I would not run blindly again. I would not be caught again. I would *not* let them drag me back behind a locked door where no one could hear me scream. I had one chance. And I would take it.

I began watching. Not in the way a wife was supposed to, not with soft eyes, not with patience or deference. I watched with purpose. Every moment of my husband's routine became a blueprint, every gesture a detail to be cataloged, every habit a piece of the map I was building in my mind.

He rose before dawn, as he always had, to lead morning prayer with the other men. He expected breakfast ready when he returned. He expected quiet when he ate. He expected his clothes folded, his boots placed by the door, his belongings exactly where he left them.

He expected *me* to be exactly where he left *me*.

And that was his mistake.

After evening supper, he would sit in the study with the others, discussing scripture, discussing discipline. I was to sit with the women, heads bowed, hands still. He believed I was still weak, still *learning*. That was his second mistake.

He would go to bed early, expecting me to follow shortly after, as I always had.

But I had been careful since the night in the pastor's house. My movements were slower, my voice softer, my obedience unquestioning. I had *learned*, not the lesson they wanted me to learn, but the lesson that would save me.

I had learned *how to disappear.*

The first thing I needed was money.

There was no currency exchanged between wives. There was no need. Everything belonged to the household, and the household belonged to the men. If I asked for anything, even something as small as a handkerchief, it would be noted. I had no accounts, no way to barter, no way to keep anything of my own.

But I had learned patience.

The wives were responsible for collecting tithes after church services, small donations placed in baskets to be counted before being given to the pastor. We handled them first. It was a task of trust. And trust could be broken.

I had never stolen before. Not because I was righteous, not because I was pure, but because I had never *needed* to. Until now. It started small, a single bill tucked into the folds of my dress, pressed flat against my stomach beneath the fabric. The weight of it sent ice through my veins, but I did not hesitate.

One bill became two. A handful of coins slipped into the lining of my apron. A little at a time. Never enough to be noticed. Never enough to raise suspicion. But enough to matter. I did not know how much I would need. I only knew that I needed *something.*

The second thing I needed was a place to go.

I had no maps, no knowledge of what lay beyond the boundary of our land. I had only what I had overheard, what I had gathered in small moments when the men spoke freely, assuming no wife would understand.

I knew there was a town beyond the hills, one far enough that no one traveled there often, far enough that it was spoken of like another world entirely. A place where women walked alone. A place where a woman like me could become no one.
That was the destination. I did not need to know what lay beyond it. I only needed to reach it.

The third thing I needed was a night.

There were few windows of opportunity in a household that never truly slept, in a community that watched over its women like shepherds guarding sheep from wolves.

But there was one night, once a month, when the men traveled beyond our settlement for a gathering. It was a night of sermons, a night of deep study, a night when they left before dark and did not return until dawn.

That was the night. I marked it in my mind. Two weeks. I had two weeks.

I moved carefully. I did not allow my hands to shake when I prepared my husband's meals. I did not allow my voice to break when I whispered scripture with the other wives. I did not allow my thoughts to wander when I sat at the sewing table, fingers working thread through cloth.

I was silent. I was still.

But I was *moving*.

At night, after my husband slept, I rehearsed. I mapped my path through the house in the dark, each step measured, each breath controlled. I counted the seconds it would take to unlatch the back door, the moments I would need to cross the yard without making a sound. I knew which floorboards creaked, which doors groaned in protest when opened too quickly. I memorized it until it became part of me. The escape lived in my bones now.

I stole other things. Small things. A roll of bread tucked beneath my sleeve. A piece of dried meat left too long in the kitchen. A scarf, worn and frayed at the edges, but enough to hide my hair, enough to make me *different* if I made it far enough.

I did not think of what would happen if I was caught. I could not afford to think of it. I only thought of the road. The town. The life waiting beyond it.

The night arrived faster than I expected.

The men left in groups, their voices low, their steps steady. I watched them from the window, my hands folded in my lap, my heartbeat measured, controlled. I waited.

I let time settle, let the darkness grow deeper, let the silence of the house press against me. Then, I moved. I did not hesitate. I did not stop.

I gathered the small bundle I had hidden beneath my sleeping mat, the weight of stolen food, stolen money, stolen *hope* pressed against me.

I stepped into the hallway, my feet knowing the way. Through the kitchen. To the back door. The latch was cold beneath my fingers. I turned it, slowly. The door opened. And I stepped into the night.

The air was cold, the sky vast and endless above me, the stars brighter than they had ever been. I had never seen them like this before, never truly *looked* at them. I had never been alone beneath them, never stood beneath the open sky without someone beside me, watching, waiting.

I did not stop. I did not *breathe*. I ran. I ran past the edge of the yard, past the fence that had always seemed so tall but now felt too small, past the last trace of the only home I had ever known. My feet hit the dirt road, and I did not look back. I did not hear anything at first. But then—

A voice. Sharp. Close. I had been seen. My stomach turned to ice. I ran faster, my breath coming in short, sharp gasps, my feet barely touching the ground. But it was too late. The footsteps were closing in. The hands reached for me.

And this time—

I did not wake from the nightmare.

Entry 20—
The Last Straw

The world snapped into focus with the sharp, stinging cold of the dirt beneath my cheek. My breath came in ragged, desperate gasps as the weight of his body pressed me into the ground, pinning me in place. My arms twisted painfully behind my back, wrists caught in a grip so tight I could feel my skin bruising beneath his fingers. I had been caught. Again. And this time, there would be no soft words, no false patience. This time, he would ensure that I learned.

The road stretched out ahead of me, empty and silent beneath the vastness of the night sky. I had almost made it past the bend, past the last shadow of the house, past the point where I could still be dragged back. But my body had betrayed me, one misstep, one breath too loud, one moment too slow. And now, here I was, my face pressed into the dust, the bitter taste of failure coating my tongue.

The grip on my arms tightened, yanking me up onto my knees. My body screamed in protest, every muscle aching, but I did not fight. There was no point in fighting now. His breath was warm against my ear, his voice steady, unshaken, terrifying in its control.

"You thought you could leave me."

It was not a question. I swallowed hard, my throat raw, my chest heaving. I did not answer.

His fingers dug deeper into my skin. "You thought you could *run from me.*"

I closed my eyes, willing my body to be still, willing the shaking in my limbs to stop, willing the fear not to show on my face. He wanted fear. He *fed* on fear. I would not give it to him. He exhaled sharply, his grip shifting as he hauled me fully to my feet. My legs buckled, my vision swimming, but I did not fall. He wouldn't let me. Not yet.

"You don't understand," he murmured, his tone almost thoughtful, almost amused. "You still think you *have* a choice."

I did not speak. He turned me roughly, gripping my jaw in one hand, forcing me to look at him. His face was calm, his eyes dark, filled with something I could not name. Not anger. Not rage. Something worse. Certainty.

"You are my wife," he said, his voice quiet, deliberate. "You belong to me."

I tried to swallow, but my throat was dry, my breath caught somewhere between my ribs. His fingers pressed harder against my skin. "You will obey me."

His gaze did not waver, did not soften.

"Or I will break you."

The words landed between us like a final blow, more brutal than any hand, more violent than any strap. I felt them settle deep into my bones, colder than the night air, heavier than the weight of his hands. There it was. The truth. The thing he had always believed, the thing I had always known but had never heard spoken aloud.

I was not a person. I was not *his wife.* I was *his possession.* And if I did not surrender completely, if I did not let him carve away the last remaining parts of myself, he would crush me until there was nothing left. My silence made him smile.

"Now you understand," he said softly.

His grip loosened just enough to let my head drop forward, my body sagging under exhaustion, under the weight of everything I could not say. He still believed he had won. He still believed he could bend me until I broke. But he was wrong. Because something inside me had already shattered. And not in the way he wanted. Not in a way that could be put back together. The fear was gone. The hesitation was gone. What was left, what remained, was something harder, sharper, something he had not expected. Hatred.

Not fear. Not obedience.

Hatred.

It burned in my chest, coiled deep in the hollow spaces where love had once lived, filling me with something colder, something stronger than I had ever known. He had made a mistake. He had pushed too far. I had always wanted to escape before. Now, I wanted to *destroy him.* But I said nothing. I only nodded, my body slack, my voice quiet. "I understand."

It was the first true lie I had ever spoken. He believed it. Because he needed to. Because he wanted to. Because men like him always believed that pain could shape a woman into something more manageable, more malleable, more *theirs.*

He did not see what he had created.

He did not know what was coming.

He released me, his touch lingering for just a moment longer, as if waiting for me to collapse completely, to surrender the last of my resistance. But I did not. I stood. I did not sway. I did not fall. And I did not let him see that, for the first time in my life, I was *not afraid of him anymore.* He would learn soon enough.

And when he did, I would not be the one who broke.

The walk back to the house was slow, deliberate. He held my arm just tightly enough to remind me of his control, his ownership, his power. My body ached, my steps were careful, but I did not let myself stumble. I would not give him that satisfaction. The fire inside me burned too hot now, too steady. I did not need to fight him tonight. That would come later.

For now, I let myself become what he wanted to see, defeated, obedient, *his*. I let my shoulders sag just enough, let my breath come shallow, let my gaze drop to the ground. It was an act, but I played it well. I had learned the rules long ago, learned how to survive by giving him exactly what he expected. But this time, it was different. This time, it was not survival I was planning. It was something else entirely.

He led me through the front door, shutting it behind us with a quiet, controlled force. The house was still, dark except for the faint glow of the kitchen lantern.

I let him steer me toward the bedroom. My skin burned beneath his touch, but I did not flinch. I did not resist.

I knew what he wanted. He had to reclaim me. He had to prove that I was still his. That I had never been anything *but* his. I let him believe it.

When he pressed his lips to my forehead, murmured something low about *forgiveness*, about *restoring what was broken*, I did not recoil. I let the moment stretch, let him feel certain, let him think that his correction had worked, that I was pliable again, emptied out and waiting to be filled with his will. I lay still beside him in bed, my breathing even, my body unmoving.

I did not sleep.

I listened to the rhythm of his breath, waiting, counting the spaces between each inhale and exhale, marking the shift when his body began to sink into deep rest. He was not worried anymore. He thought he had won. He thought I had learned my place. The fool. I had *never* been more dangerous than I was now. Because now, I was patient. Now, I was willing to wait. Now, I *knew* what I had to do.

The night stretched on, long and endless, my body curled beneath the sheets beside him, my mind sharpening like the edge of a blade.

He thought he could break me.

He thought I would surrender.

But I would never belong to him.

And the next time I left this house, I would not be coming back.

Entry 21—
Running in the Dark

The night stretched long and silent, the darkness thick and endless, pressing against the walls of the house like a warning. I lay still, my body rigid beneath the weight of the sheets, listening to the deep, steady rhythm of my husband's breath beside me. Each inhale, each exhale, measured, controlled, unbothered. He had no reason to be restless. He had no reason to be awake. He believed the lesson had been learned, that my body had finally yielded, that my will had been pressed thin enough to break.

I let him believe it.

For hours, I had not moved. I had not allowed my breathing to shift, had not allowed a single muscle to tense or twitch beneath the covers. I had waited, my eyes open in the dark, counting his breaths, marking the slow descent of his body into deep, careless sleep.

Outside, the wind howled low against the walls, rattling the shutters. The branches of the trees groaned, bending under the weight of the night. The world felt vast beyond the confines of the house, wide and open and terrifying. But I had made my choice. And this time, I would not fail.

I shifted slowly, carefully, peeling the sheets away inch by inch, my movements controlled, deliberate. My skin burned where the bruises still lingered from the last punishment, the memory of the strap carving itself into the flesh of my back, my arms. I swallowed against the ache, against the tremor of pain, forcing my body to remain steady. I could not afford weakness. Not now.

Sliding my legs over the edge of the bed, I lowered my feet to the floor, my toes barely brushing the wooden planks. The house was old, and I knew every board that groaned under weight, knew where to step, where to shift my balance. My husband stirred beside me, exhaling sharply before settling again, his body sinking deeper into the mattress.

I did not breathe.

For a long moment, I remained still, waiting, listening.

Then, I moved.

One step. Then another.

I reached for the small bundle I had hidden beneath the bed earlier that day, a few stolen scraps of food, the scarf I had taken from the pastor's wife, the handful of bills I had tucked away, each one stolen carefully, deliberately, over the last few weeks. It was not much, but it was enough. It had to be.

I crept toward the door, my fingers closing around the handle, twisting it slowly, carefully. The latch gave without protest, the door opening with only the faintest whisper of movement. I stepped into the hall, the cold air wrapping around me, sending a shiver through my limbs.

The house was silent. This was my moment.

I moved quickly now, my feet light, my breath shallow. I passed the study, the room where I had been broken and reshaped, where the pastor had pressed his hands together and told me I would never be anything but a wife, a servant, a body that existed only to be filled with obedience. I passed the gathering room, where the other women sat each day, their heads bent, their voices low, murmuring scripture, reinforcing the words that had kept us all trapped.

I reached the kitchen. The back door was only a few feet away. I had made it this far before. I had been standing in this very spot, my hand on this very latch, when he had caught me last time.

But now, I knew better. Now, I would not hesitate. I turned the handle. The door creaked. Just slightly. Just enough to send a bolt of fear through my spine. I held my breath. Waited. Nothing. I exhaled, stepping outside, closing the door behind me with careful precision.

The night was cold. The wind cut through my dress, slicing into my skin, but I did not stop to shiver, did not stop to think. I only moved. The path stretched ahead of me, dark and uneven. The road was not far. If I could reach it, if I could get past the last row of houses, past the fields beyond, I could disappear. I could find the town. I could be free.

I ran.

The night swallowed me whole.

My feet pounded against the dirt, each step pushing me farther from the house, from the life that had tried to cage me, from the man who had vowed to break me. The wind whipped through my hair, my breath coming in sharp, desperate bursts. My body screamed in protest, my muscles aching from exhaustion, from pain, from weeks of holding everything inside. But I did not stop. I did not slow.

And then—

A sound. Distant. Low. The barking of a dog.

I kept running. The barking grew louder, sharper, echoing across the open land. Then another joined in. And another. I clenched my teeth, my lungs burning. They had noticed. They knew. The house was waking up. Panic clawed at my chest, but I forced it down, forced my body forward. I was ahead. I still had time. I reached the fence at the edge of the fields, my hands gripping the wooden slats, splinters cutting into my palms. I pulled myself up, swung my legs over, landing hard on the other side, my knees buckling. I scrambled to my feet, ignoring the pain, ignoring the way my vision blurred for half a second. I ran.

Behind me, the barking grew frantic, urgent. A shout. A voice I knew too well. My husband. Then another voice. The pastor. The others were waking. I ran harder. The road was ahead of me now, the open stretch of dirt and gravel, the path that would take me away, that would take me somewhere new. Somewhere safe. Then, footsteps. Close.

Too close. I did not slow. I did not turn. But I knew. I *knew.*

The sound of heavy boots against the dirt, moving faster, closing in. My body wanted to give out, wanted to collapse, but I could not let it. Not now. Not after everything.

Then—

A hand. Gripping my arm. Yanking me back. I stumbled, my body twisting, the ground rushing up to meet me.

And then, darkness.

The impact sent a sharp, jarring pain through my body, the breath knocked from my lungs as I hit the cold, hard ground. The weight of the fall rattled my ribs, my arms, my skull, but I did not let the pain overtake me. I had no time for pain. No time for fear. No time for anything except what I had left, the desperate, raw instinct to get up. To run.

But the grip on my arm tightened, yanking me back before I could even gather my limbs beneath me. My body twisted, my heels scraping against the dirt as I thrashed against the hold, against the force dragging me down, back, back into the nightmare I had sworn I would never return to.

I had been caught.

The sound of the dogs was closer now, their barks sharp, frantic, snapping through the air like the crack of a whip. Their bodies rushed toward us, low and fast, trained to hunt, trained to retrieve, trained to find what had been lost. And I was the thing they had lost. The thing they had sent their beasts after.

I gasped for breath, my arms flailing, my hands grasping at nothing as I fought against the strength pinning me. My fingernails clawed at the dirt, at the fabric of his sleeves, at the raw, empty night around me.

"Stop fighting," my husband's voice came, breathless but steady, thick with certainty. His grip was firm, absolute, as unshakable as the scripture he had pressed into my bones since the day I had married him. "It's over."

It's over.

The words scraped through my mind, the finality of them, the surety. He believed this was the end. That I was done. That he had won. And for a moment, I almost believed it, too.
For a moment, I felt the weight of the fight drain from me, the raw exhaustion, the bruises, the aching stretch of my limbs that could no longer carry me fast enough. For a moment, I thought of the other women who had tried to leave. The ones who had been dragged back. The ones who had learned their lessons. The ones who had never tried again. But I was not them. I *would not be them.*

My breath hitched, my fingers curling into the dirt, gripping the earth beneath me as if it could somehow hold me together. My mind sharpened, focused. I did not have time for pain. I did not have time for fear. I only had time for *one more chance.*

I moved fast, before he could predict it, before his grip could tighten, before he could drag me fully to my feet. I twisted sharply, using his own force against him, wrenching my arm free with a sudden, violent pull. My body pitched forward, my knees hitting the ground, but I did not stop, did not hesitate. I shoved my shoulder into his ribs, hard, pushing him off balance, just enough. Just *enough.*

His grip slipped. And that was all I needed. I lunged.
I did not run, I *threw* myself forward, my hands slamming into the ground, my legs kicking out behind me as I scrambled up, up, up. My breath burned, my muscles screamed, but I did not listen to them. I *ran.*

I heard him curse behind me, heard the scramble of boots against dirt, heard the shouts rising from the house, from the men. I felt the weight of their fury, their determination, their belief that I was something that *belonged* to them.

I ran faster.

The road was just ahead. The dogs were coming.

I could hear their paws tearing into the dirt, could feel their snarls cutting through the air, could sense their bodies closing the distance, the heat of them, the force of them.
The road.

If I could make it to the road, I had a chance. A real one.

I forced my legs to move faster, my arms pumping, my breath ragged, my heart slamming against my ribs.

A split second before the dogs reached me, I jumped.

The fence loomed ahead, the last boundary between captivity and freedom, between *him* and *me*. I threw myself at it, my fingers gripping the top edge, splinters digging into my palms as I hauled myself up, my body screaming in protest.

The dogs snapped at my heels, their teeth catching air, missing me by inches.

I swung my leg over, barely pausing before dropping down on the other side, my knees buckling as I hit the ground hard. Pain shot through me. I ignored it.

I stumbled forward, almost falling, almost collapsing, but I didn't.
I ran.
And this time, *no one caught me.*

No hands. No voices. No weight dragging me back.

Just the sound of my own breath, my own pounding footsteps, my own life finally *mine* again.
I did not stop.

Not even when the shouts faded behind me. Not even when the barking died into the distance. Not even when I could no longer see the house, no longer feel it in my bones, no longer taste its walls in my mouth.

I did not stop.

I ran.

And I ran.

And I ran.

Until, at last, the night swallowed me whole.

And I *was free.*

Entry 22—
The Road to Nowhere

The fluorescent light buzzed overhead, flickering weakly, casting a sickly glow against the cracked tiles of the gas station bathroom. The air smelled of mildew and cleaning chemicals, a sharp contrast to the scent of dirt and sweat that clung to my skin. My fingers gripped the cold porcelain sink, my knuckles white, my breath still ragged from the night's escape.

I had made it.

For the first time in as long as I could remember, I was alone. No voices whispering scripture in my ears. No heavy hands pressing me down, forcing me into obedience. No locked doors. No *him*.

Just *me*.

I lifted my head slowly, forcing myself to look. The mirror was cracked, a deep spiderweb of fractures running through the glass. The face staring back at me was one I did not recognize. Hollow cheeks, smudges of dirt streaking my skin, lips chapped and raw, eyes wide with something between exhaustion and disbelief. My hair was tangled, hanging in uneven knots around my face, strands falling over my forehead in wild, unkempt clumps.

This was *me*.

This was what was left.

I had not seen my reflection in months. Maybe longer. There had been no mirrors in the house, none in the church, none in the places they allowed women to go. I had been told not to seek my own image, not to concern myself with vanity, with self-importance. I had learned to exist without it, to live without knowing what I looked like outside of *his* eyes, outside of what *he* told me I was.

And now, standing here, I understood why they had kept me from it. Because looking at myself now, I *saw.*

The bruises, deep and dark along my jaw, fading yellow on my arms. The sharp lines of my collarbones, the way my dress hung loose around my body, the shape of someone starved, not just for food, but for something more, something deeper. I had been *erased.* Piece by piece, they had stripped me away. But I was still *here.*

I touched my face lightly, tracing the ridge of my cheekbone, the swollen cut at the edge of my lip, the dirt pressed into the curve of my jaw.

This was *me.*

And I was still alive.

I blinked, staring at my own reflection, willing myself to believe it. My image wavered slightly in the cracked glass, the fractures splintering my face into fragments. It was fitting, really. I was a collection of broken pieces, barely held together, still shaking, still trying to make sense of what was left. My breath shuddered out, my hands gripping the sink tighter, as if letting go would send me collapsing onto the floor. My body ached, every muscle trembling, my knees weak beneath me. I had been running for hours. Days. I had lost track of time, of distance.

The last thing I remembered was the endless stretch of road beneath my feet, the sound of my own breath, the night closing in around me. I had run until my legs threatened to give out, until the pain in my ribs became unbearable, until I could no longer feel the weight of my fear pressing against my spine. I had run until I had seen the neon sign blinking in the distance, the gas station standing alone like a beacon in the dark. And I had made it inside. The attendant hadn't looked at me. No one had. That was the first sign that I had done it. That I had *escaped.* Because I had become *invisible.* A girl with no name. No past. No husband. No home. Just another stranger passing through.

I reached for the faucet, twisting the knob. A weak stream of water sputtered out, cold against my fingertips. I cupped my hands beneath it, bringing it to my face, scrubbing the dirt from my skin, letting it run down my arms, over my wrists, washing away everything that had been left behind. The water swirled dark in the sink, spiraling down the drain. *Gone.*

I breathed in, deep and slow. And then, for the first time in months, I smiled. It was small, barely there, just a ghost of movement at the corner of my lips. But it was real. Because I had done it. I was *free.* And no one would ever take that from me again. But freedom came with a price.

The gas station was quiet, save for the occasional hum of the refrigeration units, the muffled voices of people outside, the steady, rhythmic ticking of the clock mounted above the door. I didn't know how much time had passed. I had been too afraid to look, too afraid that measuring my moments here would somehow make them shorter, would remind me that this was temporary, that I could not linger.

I pressed my hands against the cold porcelain once more, grounding myself. Where would I go? I had no answers. Just the simple fact that *I could not go back.*

A knock at the door sent a jolt of terror through my body, my hands flying to my chest, my heart hammering against my ribs. I froze, waiting, barely breathing. Another knock. Not pounding. Not demanding. Just a soft, hesitant tap. My breath shuddered out of me, my limbs shaking. Someone was waiting. Maybe they needed the bathroom. Maybe they had barely even noticed me. Maybe it was *him.*

I reached for the lock, my fingers shaking. My mind screamed at me to move, to run, to *get out now* before it was too late. The knock came again. I squeezed my eyes shut, pressing my forehead against the cool glass of the mirror. I had come this far. I had made it out. Now I had to figure out how to *stay* free.

The knocking came again, soft, almost hesitant, but it sent a bolt of terror down my spine. My breath caught, my body instinctively curling in on itself, every muscle coiled tight, ready to run, ready to fight, ready to *survive*. I was not safe. Not yet.

I turned slowly, my back pressing against the cold porcelain sink, my gaze locked on the door as if my sheer will could hold it shut. The fluorescent light above flickered again, buzzing faintly, casting long, uneven shadows along the cracked tile floor. I tried to steady my breathing, tried to remind myself that it could be nothing. Just another traveler. Just a stranger waiting their turn.

But my body *knew* better. Because I had lived in fear for too long. Because I had been hunted before. Because I had seen what happened to women who were caught.

I swallowed hard, my fingers twitching at my sides. My clothes were still damp with sweat, my body still aching from the run, the bruises along my arms and ribs a constant reminder of what I had left behind.

I couldn't go back. I wouldn't. I needed to move. I needed to *think*.

The gas station was mostly empty. I had been careful, slipping in unnoticed, my head down, my body small. The attendant hadn't even looked at me when I'd ducked inside, his eyes glassy with boredom, one hand idly flipping through a magazine behind the counter.

Had someone seen me anyway? Had someone *recognized* me?

A thousand thoughts raced through my mind in the span of a breath. Had he found me already? Had he sent someone? Were the men from the church already closing in, preparing to drag me back, to make an *example* of me? I had seen what happened to women who ran. I *knew* what happened to women who ran.

My breath came too fast, too shallow, my pulse hammering behind my ribs. The air inside the bathroom was too thin, the walls too close. The cracked mirror reflected back the terror in my eyes, the wildness in my expression.

I had to *move.*

I reached for the small bundle I had carried with me, my stolen scraps of food, the few crumpled bills that had been hidden beneath my dress. It wasn't much, but it was all I had. My fingers closed around the fabric, my heart pounding in my ears as I backed toward the farthest wall, pressing myself into the cold tile, bracing for whatever was coming next.

The knocking stopped. A long silence stretched between me and whoever stood beyond the door. And then, footsteps. Moving away. I let out a shaky breath, my entire body trembling. I could barely feel my legs beneath me, barely register the ache in my ribs, the way my pulse still raced. Had it just been a stranger? Had I imagined it? Or had someone decided I wasn't worth the trouble, yet?

I stayed still for another moment, straining to hear, to *listen.* Nothing but the hum of the refrigeration units in the distance, the faint murmur of a television playing somewhere in the station. Slowly, carefully, I reached for the lock. My fingers hesitated over the metal, my breath still unsteady. I had no choice. I couldn't stay here. I had made it too far to let fear keep me trapped in this tiny, grimy gas station bathroom. I turned the lock.

The soft *click* echoed in the empty room. I pulled the door open an inch, peering through the crack. The gas station was the same as when I had entered. Dimly lit, mostly empty, the clerk still flipping through his magazine, uninterested. A lone trucker stood near the refrigerators, a bottle of soda in his grip, staring blankly at the rows of snacks. No one looked at me. No one noticed. I forced myself to breathe. I had to keep going. I couldn't afford to *stop*.

Pulling the hood of my sweater up, I adjusted the scarf I had wrapped around my neck, another stolen item, but necessary, something to cover the bruises, to make me look like *someone else*. Then, with careful, measured steps, I walked out. I did not run. I did not look back.

I moved through the aisles, my hands tightening into fists at my sides, my mind screaming at me to *hurry, hurry, hurry*, but I did not let myself rush. I reached the door.

The night stretched out beyond it, cold and vast and open. The road was still waiting for me, the unknown still ahead.

I stepped outside. The air hit my skin like ice. I kept walking. One step. Then another. And I did not stop.

Entry 23—
First Night in a Shelter

For years, I had been warned about places like thisl dark whispers from the pastor's wife, warnings laced with quiet contempt from the older women in our study groups. Shelters were where *fallen* women went, where the rebellious, the defiant, the lost ended up. They were places of filth, of sin, of women who had turned their backs on God and found themselves without protection. They spoke of these places the way they spoke of ruin, of destruction, of punishment.

I had believed them, once.

But sitting here now, on the thin mattress of a metal-framed cot, wrapped in a blanket that smelled faintly of detergent and something older, something human, something *real*, I saw the truth.

The shelter was not a place of sin.

It was a place of survival.

The room was quiet but not silent. It was filled with the kind of hushed voices that had learned to be careful, to be cautious. Women curled into themselves on their bunks, some staring at the walls, others focused on their hands, the floor, the past. Some whispered in small groups, their voices low, cautious, sharing secrets, sharing pain, sharing what had been taken from them.

I pulled the blanket tighter around me, my fingers stiff, aching. My body still had not caught up with what had happened, with how far I had run, with the fact that I had *made it*. I still expected to wake up in *his* bed, to the press of his weight beside me, to the sound of his voice telling me where I had to be, what I had to do, how I had to *be*.

But that was over. I was here. And I was not alone.

A woman sat on the bunk beside mine, her legs drawn up to her chest, her fingers picking at the hem of the sweater she wore. It was too big for her, hanging loose around her small frame, the sleeves swallowed by her hands. She had dark circles beneath her eyes, deep and hollow, the kind of exhaustion that didn't come from just a few nights of missed sleep. It was the kind that settled into your bones, the kind that never truly went away.

She looked at me, her gaze flicking over my face, my hair, the bruises that no scarf could fully hide.

"First night?"

Her voice was quiet, careful. I nodded. My throat was too tight to speak. She exhaled, nodding slightly, as if she had already known. As if it was obvious.

"We all have the same scars," she murmured, her fingers still tugging at her sweater. "Different stories. Same scars."

I swallowed, pressing my hands against my lap to keep them from shaking.

Another voice, from across the room, soft but edged with something sharper, something bitter. "Did you think you were the only one?"

I looked up.
The woman who had spoken was older, her hair streaked with gray, her eyes sharp, piercing, full of something heavy. She sat on the edge of her cot, her arms crossed over her chest, watching me the way someone watches an animal fresh out of a trap, assessing whether it will survive, whether it will *fight*.

I didn't know how to answer. Because the truth was, I *had* thought I was the only one. Not because I was special. Not because I was unique. But because *they* had made me believe it. *He* had made me believe it. That no one else had ever felt what I felt. That no one else had ever *dared*. That I was alone in my rebellion, in my doubt, in my suffering.

And yet, here I was, sitting in a room full of women with the same haunted look in their eyes, the same exhaustion in their bones. They had been me. And now, I was *them*. I forced myself to swallow, to clear the tightness in my throat.

"I don't know what I thought," I admitted finally. My voice sounded small, unfamiliar. Like it wasn't mine anymore.

The older woman exhaled through her nose, shaking her head slightly. "That's what they do," she said. "Make you think you're the only one. Make you think no one else has ever made it out. Make you think you *can't*."

Her gaze lingered on me, sharp and knowing.

"But you did."

I wasn't sure what to say to that. Because I had. But I didn't know *what* came next.

The younger woman beside me spoke again, her voice quieter this time.

"They won't stop looking for you."
I stiffened. I knew that already. I had *always* known that.

"Do they ever?" I asked.

No one answered. Because we all knew the truth. They never stopped.

The silence stretched between us, thick with the weight of things we didn't need to say. We all knew. They never stopped looking. Not really. Some men let go, some men moved on, but the ones who *believed*, the ones who had built their entire existence around control, obedience, power, *they never stopped*. They saw women as things, as possessions, and when a possession went missing, they hunted it down.

I clenched the blanket tighter around myself, my nails digging into the fabric, my knuckles white. I could still hear him in my head. The way he had spoken to me, soft when I obeyed, sharp when I questioned. The way he had whispered promises into my ear when he thought I had been molded into exactly what he wanted. *You are mine.*

The words sent a chill through me.

The older woman across from me shifted, adjusting the worn jacket draped over her shoulders. "Some of them come here," she said. Her voice was even, but there was something in her expression, something hard. "They show up. Looking for their wives. Their daughters. Their *property*."

The younger woman beside me pulled her knees tighter against her chest, her fingers still tugging at the hem of her sweater. "They lie to the police. They pretend they're worried. They say we're crazy. That we ran off in a fit of hysteria. That we're fragile." Her voice twisted on the last word, thick with something raw, something sharp.

I swallowed hard. I had heard those words before. I had *lived* them.

"You have a plan?" the older woman asked, watching me carefully.

A plan.

I exhaled slowly, staring down at my hands, at the way they trembled slightly, at the bruises that still ached beneath my skin. I had thought making it here *was* the plan. I had thought that if I could just get out, just make it somewhere *safe*, the rest would fall into place. But now, sitting here, surrounded by women who had already lived what I was just beginning to, I understood.

Escape was not the end. It was just the beginning.

And I needed to *think*.

I shook my head. "Not yet."

The older woman gave a slow nod, as if she had expected that answer. "You need to figure one out," she said. "Quick."

I looked up at her. "You?" I asked before I could stop myself. "Do you have one?"

A small, humorless smile touched her lips. "I did."

I waited for her to explain, but she didn't. She didn't have to. She was still *here*. Which meant the plan hadn't worked.

I forced myself to breathe evenly, to keep my hands steady. "What happens to the women who don't?"

She didn't answer right away.

The younger woman did.

"They go back."

The words hit like a slap. I flinched.

Back.

Back to *him*.

Back to all of it.

I had known that was the reality for some, but hearing it, *hearing* it, made something inside me recoil, made my stomach twist, made my throat tighten.

I couldn't go back.

I *wouldn't*.

Another silence settled over the room, thick with the knowledge we all shared, with the horror stories we didn't need to speak aloud. The woman beside me shifted, and I felt her gaze on me again, softer this time.

"You don't have to figure it out alone," she murmured.

I turned toward her, the words landing somewhere deep inside me, somewhere unfamiliar, somewhere I hadn't allowed myself to reach in years.

I didn't have to do it alone. That was new. That was *dangerous.* Because trusting anyone had never been safe. But then again, neither had staying. I inhaled, deep and slow. Maybe I didn't have a plan yet. But I would. Because I *had to.* Because I had *already* made it this far. And I wasn't going to stop now.

Entry 24—
Learning My Name Again

The woman at the front desk asked for my name.

For a moment, I had nothing to give her. The question sat there between us, simple, weightless in the air, as if it should have been easy. As if it should not have shattered me.

I opened my mouth, then closed it. My throat went dry. My fingers curled into the fabric of my borrowed sweater, my breath catching.

My name.

She had asked for *my name.*

Not "Mrs."

Not "wife of."

Not "property of."

Just me.

I should have known how to answer. But the truth was, I had not been just *me* in so long that I could barely remember who that was. I had a name, once. Before him. Before the church. Before I was told that my identity was something to be given up, something to be sacrificed, something to be shaped by the hands of the man God had chosen for me. Before I was told that my thoughts were dangerous, that my desires were sinful, that my purpose was not *mine* to decide.

Before I became *his.*

I could still remember the first time I signed my married name, the way the letters had felt foreign under my fingertips, the way the title *Mrs.* had sat heavy on my tongue, strange but permanent. Like a brand, a mark of ownership. He had watched me as I wrote it, a satisfied smile tugging at the corners of his mouth. I had been proud then. I had believed that taking his name was proof of something sacred, something holy, something that made me *whole.* But it had only made me smaller.

And now, sitting here, in this place of women who had learned the same hard truths I had, I realized I had forgotten what my name even *felt* like. I swallowed, my fingers tightening around the edge of the desk, my heart hammering against my ribs.

The woman waited, her gaze steady but patient. She had probably seen this before, women standing in front of her, hollowed out by years of erasure, struggling to answer the simplest question.

I closed my eyes. I forced myself to *remember.* Not the woman I had been with him. Not the woman I had been made to become. But *before.*

I saw a girl in the sunlight, feet bare in the grass, laughter bubbling from her throat. I saw a girl who had climbed trees, who had scraped her knees and skinned her elbows and did not apologize for it. A girl who had written her name in the margins of her schoolbooks, looping the letters in careful script, tracing them over and over as if she needed to see them to believe she existed.

I saw *her.*

And I spoke.

My name left my lips, quiet at first, unsure, unfamiliar. But it was *mine.* It had always been mine.

The woman nodded, her pen gliding over the page, as if nothing extraordinary had happened. As if I had not just reclaimed something I had thought lost forever.

I exhaled slowly.

The weight in my chest did not disappear, but it shifted, something loosening, something raw and aching giving way to something else. Something *new.*

I was not his.

I was not a *rib.*

I was a soul.

And I was *alive.*

Entry 25—Testimony

The room was small, dimly lit, the kind of space meant for whispered confessions and cautious admissions. A circle of metal folding chairs, their legs unsteady on the scuffed linoleum floor. A coffee pot in the corner, stale from hours of sitting. The air was thick with something unspoken, something heavy, something that pressed against my ribs as I took my seat among them.

Women filled the chairs around me. Some older, their faces lined with years of knowing, of surviving. Some younger, with eyes wide and uncertain, shoulders curled inward, bodies still waiting for the next blow, the next cruel word, the next moment of erasure. Some spoke in hushed voices, sharing in murmurs, trading pieces of their lives like fragments of broken glass. Others sat in silence, staring at the floor, lost in something only they could see.

I had been coming here for weeks now. Listening. Sitting in the back, absorbing the stories like scripture, committing them to memory. Their words had become part of me, winding through my thoughts, weaving into my dreams. Different lives. Different details. But the same story.

We all had the same scars.

I had never spoken. I had never needed to. It had been enough to listen, to *know* that I was not the only one. That I was not imagining things. That it had not been my fault.
But tonight, something felt different.

A woman had just finished speaking. Her voice had trembled as she recounted the first time she had tried to leave, how she had made it as far as a bus station before he found her, how he had smiled as he took her home, as if she were a stray animal he had generously decided to reclaim. How he had spent the next three days teaching her exactly what would happen if she ever tried again.

She was here now. But she still spoke in a whisper.

The silence that followed her story was thick, an unspoken understanding settling over the group. No one asked her for more. No one needed to. We all knew what had happened in those three days. We all knew the weight of a locked door, the sound of footsteps approaching, the way pain could become something you learned to live inside.

I felt it then, the shift inside me. The same fire that had pushed me to run, that had carried me through the night, that had burned in my chest as I scrubbed the dirt from my skin in that gas station bathroom, looking at my own face for the first time in months.

I took a breath. And then I did something I had not done before.

I spoke.

"My husband told me that obedience was love."

The words came out steady, stronger than I expected. The sound of my own voice startled me. The room went still.

I swallowed, the weight of their eyes pressing against me, but I did not stop.

"He said submission was a woman's highest calling. That the more I suffered, the more holy I became."

I let the words settle for a moment, let them sink into the air between us.

"At first, I believed him."

A woman across from me nodded slightly. She understood.

"I believed it when he corrected me. When he took things from me, little by little, my choices, my voice, my name. I told myself it was love. That he was shaping me into something better."

My hands clenched in my lap.

"But it wasn't love. And it wasn't faith. It was control."

My voice didn't waver. The words felt sharp, like they had been waiting inside me, pressing against my ribs, demanding to be set free.

"The night I ran, I could still hear him in my head," I admitted. "I kept waiting for his voice to tell me to turn around, to go back. To be *good* again."

The room was silent. Listening.

"But I didn't. I kept running. And now I'm here."

I exhaled slowly.

"For the first time, I'm here."

A murmur rippled through the room, a quiet acknowledgment. I met the gaze of the woman across from me, the older one with the knowing eyes. She nodded.
I had spoken.

And they had listened.

I let the silence settle, let the weight of my words hang in the air like the aftershock of something inevitable, something long overdue. My voice still echoed in my head, unfamiliar yet undeniable. I had spoken. I had said it out loud. Not in the frantic scrawl of a hidden journal, not in the soundless prayers I used to whisper into the darkness, not in the silent rebellion I had nursed inside my ribs for years.

I had spoken, and they had listened.

The woman across from me, the one who had nodded in understanding, leaned forward slightly. Her hands were clasped together, knuckles tight, a familiar tension in her shoulders. I recognized it. The way survival never quite leaves the body. The way trust is given slowly, carefully, in small, measured pieces. She took a breath, her lips pressing together before she spoke.

"I used to tell myself it was my fault," she said. Her voice was steady, but I could hear the tremor beneath it, the cracks in something once held too tightly. "That if I had just been a little better, a little quieter, a little *less*, he wouldn't have had to do what he did."

I swallowed hard. I knew that lie well. I had lived inside it.

Another woman shifted in her seat, her fingers running along the hem of her sweater, twisting the fabric between her hands. "I thought God wanted me to stay," she murmured. "That leaving meant turning my back on my vows, my family, my *faith.*"

A murmur of agreement swept through the room. Heads nodded. Shoulders tensed. Some women looked away, staring at the walls, at the floor, at the memories that still clung to them.

Faith had been a weapon in our stories, not a comfort. It had been something used against us, wrapped around our throats like a leash, like a noose. *God's order. God's will. God's punishment.*

I had once believed that too. I had once thought that submission was my burden to bear, my cross to carry, my path to righteousness.

I had believed it even when my body ached from his hands, even when my voice became smaller and smaller until it disappeared entirely. I had believed it even when I could no longer look in a mirror because the girl I once was had been buried beneath the life *he* had made for me.

But not anymore.

I took a slow breath, my hands pressing against my lap, grounding myself in the present, in the *now*. "They teach us that love is obedience," I said softly. "That faith is suffering." I looked up, meeting the eyes of the women around me. "But that's not faith. That's not love."

The woman beside me, the one who had spoken first, let out a slow exhale. "No," she said quietly. "It's not."

There was another silence then, but it was different now. It wasn't the heavy kind, the suffocating kind that filled the space between unspoken horrors and shared trauma. It was lighter. Something shifting. Something *breaking*.

We had all been told the same story, in different voices, in different words, in different homes. And we had all believed it, until we didn't.

Now, we were here. And for the first time, I was not afraid of what came next. I had survived. I had spoken. And I would never be silent again.

Entry 26—
The Final Entry

I had been writing for as long as I could remember.

In childhood, my diary had been a place of soft secrets, of prayers and wishes, of dreams too fragile to be spoken aloud. As a girl, I had pressed my thoughts into the pages like dried flowers, hopeful and innocent, believing the world was large and full of endless paths waiting to be walked.

Then I became a wife.

And my writing became something else entirely.

At first, I wrote to remind myself of the love I had promised, the devotion I was told to cultivate, the life I was meant to shape my body around like a second skin. I wrote scriptures and submission. I wrote gratitude when I did not feel it. I wrote my sins so I would not forget to repent for them.

Later, I wrote to remember the parts of myself that were slipping away. I wrote in the margins of cookbooks, in the quiet spaces between sermons, in the notebooks I hid beneath the bed, beneath the loose floorboard, beneath the weight of my own fear. I wrote the things I could not say, the thoughts I could not hold in my mind for too long without risking my own survival. I wrote the truth. And now, my truth had come to its final page.

I sat on the edge of the bed in the small shelter room, my fingers tracing the spine of the worn, weathered journal, the one I had carried with me through every step of my escape. The pages were filled with me, my anger, my fear, my rebellion, my pain.

Everything he had tried to take from me lived here, pressed between ink and paper, the last remnants of a girl who had been told she belonged to a man who never deserved her.

I turned to the final blank page. My hand did not shake as I wrote the words. He told me I was his. He was wrong. The sentence sat there, bold and defiant, a statement, a declaration, a truth I had come to know in every aching bone, every breath of freedom, every step I had taken away from him. I did not belong to him. I never had. I closed the journal, the weight of it settling in my lap. I knew what I had to do.

I stood, crossing the room, my feet steady on the wooden floor. The small window was open just enough to let in the cool air, the scent of the city beyond it, the sound of a world still moving, still turning, still existing beyond the walls that had once held me prisoner.

The metal wastebasket sat beside the bed, empty except for a few crumpled papers, remnants of past tenants, past lives that had passed through this space before me. I reached into my pocket, fingers closing around the small box of matches I had taken from the shelter's communal kitchen. For a moment, I hesitated. Not out of fear. But because I wanted to remember this moment. I wanted to remember what it felt like to choose, fully and completely, to erase the past not out of shame, but out of defiance. I struck the match.

The small flame flickered to life, fragile but unyielding.

I pressed it to the first page of the journal, watched as the fire took hold, as the edges curled and blackened, as the ink blurred and disappeared beneath the growing flames. I dropped it into the wastebasket, and the fire consumed it. The words I had written, the fears I had carried, the lies I had been told and the truths I had uncovered, they all turned to ash. I did not need them anymore. Because I was still *here*.

And I was free.

I turned away before the flames died, before the last embers faded into nothing. I walked to the door, my hand resting on the handle for just a moment. I had been told this world would destroy me. That without him, I would crumble. That without the structure of obedience, I would be lost. That without a man to guide me, I would have no purpose, no direction, no future. But I was still standing. And the world was waiting. I opened the door. And I walked into it.

The night air was different now.

Before, when I had run, the darkness had been suffocating, filled with shadows that felt like hands reaching for me, branches clawing at my arms, whispers of his voice curling around my throat like smoke. The night had been a thing to fear, a reminder that I was small, that I was being hunted, that there was no world beyond the one I had fled, only an endless stretch of nowhere, waiting to swallow me whole.

But now, standing outside the shelter, the city stretching ahead of me in blinking lights and distant sounds, the air felt open, wide, full. The dark no longer pressed against me. It did not belong to him. It belonged to *me*.

I pulled my borrowed jacket tighter around my frame, feeling the weight of it settle against my shoulders. It wasn't mine. Nothing I owned had come with me. The dress I had worn the night I ran had been thrown away, left behind in a garbage bin behind a truck stop, like a shedding skin I never wanted to wear again. The scarf, the sweater, the shoes, they were all given to me by women who had once stood exactly where I stood now. Women who had left everything behind and stepped into a world that had once seemed impossible.

I stepped off the curb, my feet landing on the cracked pavement, solid beneath me. I did not have a destination. I did not have a plan. But for the first time in my life, that did not scare me. For so long, my life had been dictated by rules, by expectations, by the steady, unwavering path that had been laid before me before I was even old enough to understand that I had never chosen it. My days had been mapped out, my purpose decided, my body and mind trained to fit into the narrow space they had carved for me.

A good wife. A faithful woman. A servant to a god I had never been allowed to question, to a husband I had never been allowed to deny. For years, my future had belonged to them. Now, it belonged to me.

The city breathed around me, alive in a way I had never known. A car passed, headlights sweeping across my face, and I did not flinch, did not duck, did not shrink away from being seen. I walked, slow at first, my body still learning what it meant to move without direction, without permission, without the weight of someone else's will pressing against my spine.

I did not know where I would sleep. I did not know where I would go. But I *knew* one thing. I would never return.

A bus station sat ahead, a flickering sign casting a dull glow onto the sidewalk. A few people sat on benches, their heads low, their shoulders curved inward, the quiet patience of people waiting for something, transportation, movement, change. I could be one of them. I could buy a ticket, board a bus, let it carry me to a place I had never been before.
Or I could keep walking, let my feet carry me wherever they wanted to go, let the night unfold before me in ways I had never been allowed to imagine. It didn't matter.

Because I was *choosing*.

I stopped in front of the station, my breath misting in the cold. I reached into my pocket, feeling the crumpled bills I had stolen, my fingers brushing over them, the last remnants of a past life that had tried to bury me.

I thought about the journal I had burned, the words that had turned to smoke, the pages curling into ash. He had told me I was *his*. But he had been wrong. He had always been wrong.

I was mine. And no one would ever take that from me again. I exhaled, steady and slow, then took a step forward. And I did not look back.

Epilogue

The story you have just read is fiction, but it is not fantasy. The walls of the world the protagonist fled from still stand, its doors still lock, its rules still govern the lives of countless women and girls who do not have the privilege of escaping into the freedom of a secular society. What begins as love, devotion, and faith too often twists into something else, submission without limits, silence without choice, suffering without dignity. The nature of Christian fascist marriage is not about love. It never was. It is about control. And in control, love withers into obedience, obedience curdles into violence, and violence is justified in the name of God.

Christian patriarchal movements do not advertise themselves as theocratic cults or authoritarian traps. They do not lead with whips and chains but with honey and open arms, promising purpose, belonging, and divine favor. They tell young women, hungry for meaning and stability, that they are part of something greater, that submission is sacred, that a husband is the earthly extension of God's will. They cite scripture, praising the Proverbs 31 woman who "rises while it is yet night," who "opens her mouth with wisdom and the teaching of kindness," who is never idle, never resistant, never unruly. They declare that men are ordained to rule, and women to serve, as naturally as the sun rises and sets. This is the promise, and for many, it is intoxicating.

But what happens after the doors close and the wedding guests leave? What happens when a woman realizes that her dreams have been swallowed whole by the institution she was told would fulfill her? The women who find themselves trapped within these systems often do not see the bars until it is too late. Christian fascist marriage is an empire of expectations: it controls what women wear, how they speak, what they read, whom they associate with. It rewires their thoughts, recasting doubt as sin, unhappiness as rebellion, pain as sanctification. It binds them to their husbands legally, financially, spiritually, and socially, ensuring that the act of leaving is not simply difficult but unimaginable. In some cases, a woman does not even have the right to her own money, her own body, or her own children. She has been trained to believe that escape is failure, that seeking freedom is not just betrayal but damnation.

These conditions are not unique to one sect, one time period, or one nation. The oppression of women in the name of faith is a global phenomenon, a throughline stretching across centuries and cultures. In the United States, the resurgence of Christian nationalist movements has emboldened politicians to legislate women's bodies, to roll back their autonomy, to enshrine a vision of marriage that more closely resembles ownership than partnership. The erasure of reproductive rights, the criminalization of bodily autonomy, and the glorification of submissive womanhood are all part of the same effort: to ensure that women remain tethered to roles they did not choose, to strip them of the ability to control their own futures, to reduce them to vessels and servants.

It would be a mistake to believe this is about faith alone. Christian fascism does not emerge in a vacuum, it is not solely the domain of religious extremists, but of power-hungry men who see faith as the most convenient leash with which to control women. It is not Christ they follow but the consolidation of power through manufactured moral panic, through the selective application of scripture that justifies their rule while condemning any challenge to it. They invoke God when convenient, abandon him when necessary, and manipulate his words to serve their interests. It is no coincidence that the very men who demand the strictest adherence to biblical womanhood rarely apply those same standards of virtue, humility, and sacrifice to themselves.

For many women, the realization that Christian fascist marriage is a cage does not come all at once but in increments, in small betrayals, in lingering doubts, in quiet moments of suffocation. It may be the first time they are told they cannot leave the house without permission. It may be the first time they are hit and then told that the Bible commands their endurance. It may be the birth of a daughter, the sudden, horrifying recognition that their child will be raised in the same system, with the same chains, with even fewer chances of escape. And for those who do try to leave, the journey is not easy. The world outside is foreign, filled with fears deliberately planted by those who kept them captive. Women who flee these marriages face exile from their communities, loss of their children, financial ruin, and sometimes, the most brutal consequence of all, death at the hands of the man who once swore to love them.

There is a reason that patriarchal religious sects place such a high premium on women's purity, obedience, and silence: because they understand that women, when free to think, to question, to act, are a direct threat to their power. The entire system hinges on women believing that they are meant to serve, that their existence is justified only in relation to the men who rule over them. The moment a woman begins to question, the moment she refuses to submit, the illusion fractures. That is why these systems punish women who rebel, shame women who think, and rewrite history to erase women who have led revolutions of their own.

The protagonist of this book represents more than just one woman, she represents countless women who have found themselves trapped in lives that were never truly theirs. She represents the women who whisper doubts in the dark but cannot yet speak them aloud. She represents those who have fled and those who still remain, held in place by fear, by loyalty, by the weight of indoctrination. And most importantly, she represents hope, the hope that escape is possible, that freedom is worth fighting for, that no matter how deep the indoctrination, no matter how total the control, the human spirit still strains against its bonds.

Christian fascist marriage is a horror story not because it is filled with shadows and ghosts but because it is real. It is the woman in Texas denied medical care for a miscarriage. It is the teenage girl married off to a church elder three times her age. It is the mother of four who stays with a violent husband because her pastor tells her that leaving would damn her to hell. It is the girl who grows up believing that her worth is in her silence, her purity, her ability to endure. It is a horror story with millions of protagonists, some of whom escape, many of whom do not.

And so, to the reader who recognizes themselves in these pages, to the one who has felt the walls closing in, who has wondered if there is life beyond the cage, let this book serve as both warning and invitation. Warning, because the chains will only tighten if you let them. Invitation, because beyond those chains, there is a world waiting, a world where your body is your own, your thoughts belong to no one but yourself, and your worth is not measured by your obedience to men who were never gods. Escape is difficult. It is terrifying. It comes with risks. But it is possible. And more than that, it is necessary.

For those who have already broken free, for those who fight to keep others from falling into the same trap, for those who are working every day to dismantle the systems that have claimed so many lives, know this: the house of Christian fascism is built on fear, but fear is a fragile foundation. It cannot stand forever. The more women speak, the more they resist, the more they refuse to comply, the closer it comes to collapse. And when it does, when the walls fall, when the doors swing open, when the doctrine of submission is buried in the rubble of history, there will be no mourning. There will only be relief. There will only be freedom. There will only be the voices of women who were never meant to be silent.

About EATMS Productions

What's happening to women now is not random. It's structural.

Policy, culture, technology, and power are moving in the same direction.

EATMS maps them clearly and shows how to respond.

This title is part of an ongoing body of work. All EATMS Productions titles, across all series, authors, and formats, are components of a single connected project.

Start here: EATMS System Primer — Free Bundle
https://eatms.gumroad.com/l/dyvzbw

For full catalog or inquiries: eatms.me

Free survival booklet + EATMS updates: email "EATMS" to eatms@pm.me

Please feel free to burn part or all of this book, safely, as an effigy.

www.ingramcontent.com/pod-product-compliance
Lightning Source LLC
LaVergne TN
LVHW051002080826
845145LV00009B/2411